I0831945

DOUGLAS DONASCIMENTO

SOCIAL

A CAUTIONARY NOVEL

SoCIAL - A Cautionary Novel
by Douglas DoNascimento.

Edited by	James Mayfield and Nicole DoNascimento
Published by	Briggs & Schuster
	BSA.IM

Contact information:
contact@bsa.im
Library of Congress Cataloging-in-Publication is available
ISBN: 978-0-9835120-6-6

Printed in the United States of America

To all that supported me on this creation.

CHAPTER 1

Midnight Havoc

Taylor Wins breathed the dry night air, listening to the hum of activity around the base. He hadn't spoken to his wife and child in a couple hours, and he missed them already. Debra had cried on the Skype call, but Shannon was a trooper.

Home was his reason. Those two girls, his wife and child, were his reason.

Taylor took another deep breath and nodded to himself.

There were a few soldiers playing cards nearby. Things got tough in Syria, but they had their morale to get them by. They were a family out here.

"Hey Jackson, how you doing?" Lieutenant Mayfield ambled by with a grin, talking to one of the four card players at the fold-out table.

Jackson gave a sly smile and swatted a fly away from her face. "How YOU doing?" She asked, with that typical southern sass. The men and women chuckled and one of the soldiers slapped down his cards.

"Poker!" He yelled it and the others shared quizzical glances.

"What ya mean, *poker*?" Jackson asked, and folded, tossing her own hand down on the table.

"I mean that's a full house. I win the game. That's *poker*." The soldier replied with a smug look.

"So?" Jackson pushed the chips, bottle caps actually, toward him. "It's not Gin or Snap. You don't have to shout *poker*, ya fool."

"Maybe I wanna shout…"

Taylor inhaled and grimaced at the grit of dirt between his teeth. He rolled his tongue around and spat it out.

He blocked out the mini-argument at the table. It was inconsequential, but it was a nice background hum. There was movement in the dark and he perked up. He squinted through the night, and a snake slid through the sands nearby.

Just another critter in the wild. Only things that moved out there were snakes, lizards and people with guns.

There were stars in the inky sky, twinkling down benevolently, unaware of the trouble on Earth. Wars, strife, innocents decapitated. All as a warm wind twirled mini-cyclones in the desert.

Taylor leaned back again and flexed his hands. This was ridiculous. He was too jumpy and that wasn't his style. But there was something in the night air, something strange he couldn't quite place his finger on.

A smell. Or maybe it was a feeling. He was on edge, the hairs on the back of his neck stood up.

"Still, why shout *poker* if that's not what you do? It's not polite." Jackson wouldn't let it slide.

"Who cares about polite?"

"Apparently, you don't," Jackson quipped and the others chuckled.

Taylor moved off a few paces and brought out the satellite phone. He dialled the number and waited for the phone to ring. He needed this more than he'd needed anything before. If he could speak to him and find a way out, he'd be home before the month was out.

He'd give anything to be with his wife and daughter again.

"You gonna hog that phone?" Corporal Al Majed strolled up, kicking up dust with his combat boots, his ever-present cigarette hanging from the corner of his mouth. Luckily there were no senior officers around to call him out on it; the man was a walking chimney. Majed, a graduate in linguistics, dark-skin descendant of Ethiopia, spoke eight languages including the needed local dialects.

"What, you wanna call somebody?"

Majed flashed a grin. "Ya think, Captain Obvious?"

"I'll be done in a couple." Taylor nodded at Majed's humor, but the heavy smoker didn't mosey off. He settled in for the wait, gripping the cancer stick between his two fingers and drawing the smoke into his lungs.

He huffed it out again, formed an 'o' and attempted shapes, but it came out in a stream and he swore under his breath.

Taylor cleared his throat and Majed cocked an eyebrow. "Sup?"

"Kinda need some privacy on this one, man."

Majed laughed and flicked his cigarette butt off into the dirt.

"Ya know, talking dirty with the wife doesn't count as an important call."

"Yeah, I told you that last week," Taylor replied, and punched his buddy in the arm. They'd been deployed together several times. When the situation got rough, they'd have each other's backs, but during their spare time, man, it was like being in a boy's school all over again. Hazing nonstop.

Majed stared at him a moment longer, patting his pockets for his pack and lighter. The tang of sweat, smoke and day-old cologne drifted toward him.

"This is important."

"All right, all right," Majed said, abandoning his quest for the pack. He raised his hands and backed off. "I surrender."

BOOM.

The ground shuddered. The building nearby exploded in a spray of rubble and dust.

Bodies flew through the air. Jackson collided with Taylor's side and he rolled out of the way. He turned to check on her, but half her face was a bloodied mess. Her limbs were at odd angles.

"Jackson," he said, pressing his two fingers to her blood-coated neck. There wasn't a pulse.

Under attack. His heart pounded and his breath came in ragged gasps.

Taylor rose into a crouch and looked both ways, but the haze of dust was too thick. He didn't call out - who knew what waited in the dark? Shadowy shapes darted to and fro. The pop of gunfire was close.

"What just happened?" Majed yelled in the darkness. "What's going on?"

Taylor sprinted and skidded through the rubble, coming to a halt at Majed's side. Majed was trapped, a large chunk of the building had crashed into him.

"Quiet," Taylor said, then thumbed back the man's eyelids and held up his index finger. "Follow this with your eyes." He moved his finger from side-to-side and Majed did as he was told.

He was all right.

"Can't hear a thing," Majed said loudly.

Taylor pressed the same two fingers to his lips, and the other soldier nodded. They shifted a piece of rock off his leg together, and Majed grunted and whispered, "Gotta regroup with the others. Get weapons. Gotta be an ambush of some kind."

Explosions rocked the base. A car's engine growled to life. Wordless screams echoed in the desert.

Taylor tugged the man to his feet, burying panic, tapping into that core he'd perfected during training.

Majed tested his weight on his left leg, then winced and shook his head. He slung his arm around Taylor's shoulder and they set off.

They ducked down low and limped for his room. His weapons were in there. All he had on him was a handgun, but he drew it and Majed did the same.

Their heads swivelled, searching for survivors or attackers. But there was no one in sight.

"Who is it?" Majed murmured, his brown eyes clouded with pain.

"Gotta be the Islamic State." Taylor's reply fell on deaf ears, but it felt good to say it out loud.

The base was under attack, that was all that mattered.

ISIS or whoever would pay.

The poker players were silent. A chunk of debris had split the table in two. A soldier was face down in the dirt. The back of his skull was gone.

Taylor didn't register nausea. He kept going. Gunfire sputtered through the night. Bursts of light and earth-shaking explosions followed. It didn't end. There was smoke and dust everywhere. Screams.

Where were the others? Why hadn't any of the troops mobilized to stop this?

Majed wheezed and stumbled, and Taylor strained to hold him upright. They were too slow for this. That gunfire was around the corner, behind them. A man shouted in the dark.

"Not much further," he muttered to Majed, who watched his lips and nodded through a squint.

There!

They darted toward the low-slung barracks, pockmarked with holes. Bullet casings were strewn on the ground among the corpses of men and women they'd lived with, eaten with, talked to.

The coast was clear.

They hobbled forward like a four-legged creature, scanning with its two heads, tracking through the dust. Majed stifled a sneeze. There were muffled footsteps ahead and they froze.

Taylor checked the safety on his gun: it was off.

A small contingent of soldiers rounded the corner up ahead.

He opened his mouth to call out to them. Bullets zipped past his ear, and he dropped to the ground, pulling Majed down with him.

The heavy rain of gunfire tore through the soldiers, ripping at their bodies. The sick pop of bullets entering flesh permeated his senses.

This was the day he'd die. But he wouldn't go down without a fight.

Taylor rolled onto his back and brought his gun up, searching for someone to shoot.

Majed groaned beside him, and gave a wet hacking cough. That wasn't good.

"Spread out," a voice with a thick accent said, "neutralize the rest. No prisoners for now."

Majed groaned again, but Taylor remained still. He whispered, "Quiet. They'll kill you if they find you." The other man couldn't hear him. He groaned again and louder this time, boots scuffing against the dirt.

Taylor closed his lids so he'd seem unconscious to anyone who cared to look. Majed shuffled, puffing dust, and rose to his knees. "Taylor," he groaned, "we gotta keep moving. They'll find us." He swayed slightly, and his eyes were shut. Blood streamed from a gash along his forehead.

"Taylor, where are you man?"

"There!" the man with the accent called. The crunching of boots approached. "This one lives."

"No," Taylor said, through gritted teeth. "No." He strained with the gun, to lift it, but anything he did now would result in death. If he tried to shoot, they'd kill him first.

There had to be a way to take out the man in charge.

"Gotta get outta here," Majed repeated, then struggled to stand, placing his hand flat in the dust and trying to force himself upward. "Wins, you'd better speak." The words came out garbled and Majed ejected a gob of blood from between stained lips.

The enemy wasn't in Taylor's line of sight. He couldn't fire on them without revealing his presence.

"Duck down," he whispered, pleading with his companion. Majed was a joker, he had a young wife. He liked Cuban cigars and ate double helpings of everything he could get his hands on.

He lived in Coppell too. Came over for dinner on Sundays.

Please, God. Please let him get down. Taylor swallowed hard, panic rising in his chest, forming an iron band across his ribs.

That was his brother over there.

"Kill that one."

No!

Pop, pop, pop.

The bullets came fast, tore into Majed and blood spattered the sand behind him. He screamed out loud. He fell, back arched. He hit the ground with a thud and didn't move again.

Taylor's insides twisted with regret. He should've moved. He should've saved him.

He was a coward, he didn't deserve life.

"That's all of them?" Said the man with the thick accent.

"Yes." There was a pause, the smell of copper pennies filled Taylor's nostrils. "Shoot the ones on the ground in case they live." The owner of that voice, the leader, drew closer.

This was his chance. He'd die, but he'd take this bastard down with him. Avenge what he'd done wrong.

He waited, fingers itching on the cool metal of the trigger. The man with the automatic stopped in front of him and raised it. He wasn't the leader, but one of the men under him. He wore a white balaclava with a black headband, toting the symbols of the Islamic State. His eyes were harder than a thousand deaths.

He'd have to do. No time left.

The insurgent pointed the weapon at Taylor.

Taylor's arm snapped upward. He squeezed the trigger three times. Three shots as revenge for Corporal Majed. One in the arm, one in the heart, one in the head.

The terrorist jerked, firing involuntarily. Bullets peppered the sand beside Taylor's head.

A boot crashed down on Taylor's wrist and his hand sprang open. He stared down the cool barrel of the gun.

"Leave him." A dark figure walked by, squelching in the flow of blood. American blood from American soldiers. "Let this one live." He spoke in that thick accent, Syrian. ISIS insurgent?

"Why?" The gun trembled, a bead of sweat rolled down the finger on the trigger.

But the leader stalked off without an answer, trailing blood and doom.

Taylor didn't beg for life. He accepted what was to come, but his last thoughts went home, back to his family, to his wife and little girl.

The gun fired and he was engulfed in pain.

This was the end.

CHAPTER 2

The Army Wife

"How are you holding up, Honey?"

Mrs. Perks peered through the window at her, a sympathetic grin plastered on her face, as thick and disingenuous as the fuchsia blush she'd slathered on her cheeks.

"I'm fine." That was a blatant lie. Debra ground her teeth - a habit the dentist scolded her for, frequently. No, she wasn't fine, she was anything but fine.

"Honey," the middle-aged woman answered, leaning through the window, curls illuminated by the orange ball in the sky. "It's okay to break down about it. This is your first time, it's going to be difficult." She reached out and patted her a few times; those wrinkled hands were like claws.

"Thanks Madeline, but I don't feel like breaking down, especially not with Shannon in the house." Debra answered.

Mrs. Perks gave a nod of approval and sniffed. "I remember my first time. It was difficult being away from him, running the house on my own, but I realized that it was totally up to me and it spurred me on."

Totally up to her. Debra swallowed and placed a dish in the drying rack. Did she have the strength to run their little family on her own in his absence?

Their life hadn't been the American dream they'd envisioned, but Debra and Taylor Wins had made a comfortable home on that army base in Coppell, Texas.

"What's that smell?" Mrs. Perks wriggled her nose and quirked her pencilled eyebrows.

There was a roast in the oven – she'd gone all out for the first time since he'd left, as a reminder of what it would be like when he returned. Shannon would love it and Debra could play the housewife, even though the house was without her husband.

It was a pale imitation of a good day.

Mrs. Perks cocked her head to the side, waiting for an answer. "Smells like roast turkey and potatoes."

"I thought I'd make something special tonight."

"Tonight indeed." The woman's expression turned smug and Debra frowned.

"What do you mean?" She ran the dish towel between her fingers, tracing the square pattern of threads in the material.

"Dear, it's past six. It will be hours before that bird is done yet. Past Shannon's bedtime, even." Mrs. Perks restrained a snicker and pity slid in to replace the original sympathy.

Anger flared up inside Debra's gut.

The interfering biddy always had to force her input on the

wives of the base. She thought she was better, more experienced, used to the sorrow of being alone. As if that was a good thing. She wore solitude like a badge of honor, hell, she probably didn't like it when her husband was home.

"Need me to come in and sort it out? Help you with the dishes so you can put your feet up? I'm sure I could rustle up a couple of the girls to help me out."

Debra swallowed. She could picture it: the wives crawling over the house, rifling through everything. Nothing would be safe, not even her Facebook profile.

"I've got it all under control." Debra replied, sweet as apple pie.

"If you say so," Mrs. Perks paused and flashed her yellowing teeth again. "I'll leave you to your dinner prep and be on my way." She grasped Debra's arm and patted it three times – kind of like a pet dog. "If you need anything at all, you know where to find us."

'Us' was the association of wives which roamed the base. The army wives who waited for their husbands to return and who generally meant well but poked their noses in everywhere.

Mrs. Perks gave a final wave and departed, leaving a wake of musky perfume. She didn't mean well at all. She meant to take over and control and interfere in general. Debra coughed on the cloying aftertaste of her presence.

She turned back to the oven and considered it, tapping her thumb on her chin.

Debra knew where to find the army wives. The knowledge

was an annoyance and a comfort. Taylor's absence scared her. She wasn't strong enough to handle this, and Shannon, on her own, but she wasn't used to the level of community on the base.

Here, family business was base business. Nothing was sacred.

She stood over the kitchen sink and took a moment to look out at the flowers blooming in her front yard. Beyond her begonias and sunflowers there were children playing in the street under the watchful eyes of their mothers. The sun had started to set, casting shades of orange and pink over the streets and gardens.

It was so suburban, so surreal.

How could they be happy and free when her world crumbled around her ears. She grabbed a kitchen towel, wiped her face and placed the towel on the white windowsill.

Debra sighed as she watched them. It was a warm Sunday evening. The community was in relatively good spirits considering some of the husbands had been deployed a few weeks ago. No word had been heard from them yet.

This was the first time she'd experienced this situation after years of comforting anxious wives.

A breeze brushed her auburn hair into her face. She saved her wet lashes from the attacking strands by tucking them behind her ear, then gripped the dishtowel again.

"Mom, may I have another juice?" Shannon's cute squeak stirred her from distant thoughts. She stopped obsessively rubbing her hands in the blue dish towel and turned.

Debra exhaled slowly then replied, "Umm, sure Honey. Just

give me a minute. I'll bring it out to you, okay?"

Shannon was four years old, going on five, but Debra was convinced her daughter had been born with a cache of wisdom she'd yet to share.

Shannon narrowed her eyes and tilted her head to the side. Those big brown eyes peered right into Debra's core. It amused her and made her a little uneasy. She must've been satisfied with whatever she found there, because she turned on her heels and skipped back into the living room without another word.

The antics of her little girl were always a joy.

But Taylor wouldn't be home anytime soon to share their cutie's behavior. He was far off, invisible to her now, and it made the days and nights too long. Tears pricked her eyes and she slapped them away in her frustration. What would the other wives say if they saw her like this?

It was no time to wallow; especially not in front of Shannon. She inhaled sharply and walked over to the refrigerator. It was time to be a good mom and a good wife, even if that meant she didn't get to see Taylor for a while.

At least they could Skype every other night. As long as he was safe. "Dear God, please let him be safe," she offered the silent prayer to the roof, then opened the steel door of the fridge.

She swiped the apple juice from the side compartment and popped the straw inside the juice box. It made a strangely satisfying sound when she punctured its top.

Shannon cried out, “Mommy! Mommy! Look, it’s Daddy on the TV.”

Waves of excitement washed over her, followed by a surge of dread. When army personnel were on the television it was either good news or …

Her heart pounded against her ribs. She bolted from the kitchen toward her daughter’s voice. The hall became a long blur of slow motion activity and she grappled with the walls, pushing herself forward, knocking pictures down.

It had to be good news. He had to be okay. Had to be okay.

Shannon’s little head of brown curls bounced as she jumped with glee in front of the TV. Usually Dora the Explorer aired at this time, but the show had been interrupted with a ‘Breaking News’ bulletin.

Shannon turned, her face alight with excitement and hope. “He’s on the TV, Mommy! He’s on the TV.”

“I see that,” Debra answered, then stroked her hopping head.

“Mom?”

Shannon’s questions faded into white noise. Debra’s focus was pinned on the screen. The juice box dropped to the floor and burst open. Fluid spread in a pool around her feet.

Taylor was dead.

“Mommy, you spilled the juice.” Shannon stopped bobbing up and down, and stared at the floor with a small frown. “And it was apple juice, too.”

“Oh my God.” She couldn’t let her daughter see this. Debra grabbed for the remote, but it was nowhere to be seen. She searched the coffee table and the top of the TV.

A small contingent of U.S. soldiers dispatched to Syria to settle the unrest among the Yazidi locals has been destroyed in a suspected attack by Islamic State militants. Our local correspondent in the field is there to report.

"What does co-tijet mean, Mommy? Is Daddy coming home soon?" Shannon tugged on her sleeve.

Debra found the remote on the couch and muted the TV.

Destroyed, they'd been destroyed. How did they know for sure that he was dead? That any of them were dead? There had to be some kind of proof.

Why had Taylor's face been up on the screen? Why his face specifically?

Surely they had pictures of the other soldiers in his unit.

"Mommy?"

Her beautiful child stood beside her and tears burst from the corners of Debra's eyes. How was she going to tell her baby girl?

"I can't do this," she whispered it and Shannon jostled closer. She took her mother's hand and stared up into her face, concern spreading a frown between the freckles.

A knock sounded at the front door.

"Baby, go get a kitchen towel and clean up this juice. Don't worry about me, I just miss your Daddy." Her voice cracked, and Shannon jogged away without another word.

A good little girl. Her Daddy's girl.

"I can't do this alone, Taylor." Debra was lost, swimming in a sea of agony and fear. She couldn't be without him, she couldn't function without him. What would become of her and Shannon?

That knock rapped its way into her consciousness.

She reluctantly walked to the front door, turning her back on the TV, but glancing at it over her shoulder. His face was up again.

Why? They kept putting it up, they kept showing him. There had to be some relevance to that and it scared her.

"Debra?" Mrs. Perks' voice called, "Debra are you all right?"

The knock grew more insistent.

She had to answer it.

The High School Student

There was a major construction project going on in her head.

Hailey opened her eyes but forced them closed again, swiftly. The sunshine pouring through her bedroom window had aggravated the invisible dude holding the jackhammer against her forehead.

Burying her head in her pillows and wrapping herself in a sheet cocoon offered a little reprieve. The relief was short-lived.

A few minutes passed and her alarm blared to life.

The construction work reached a crescendo. The last 24 hours had been hellish for Hailey. Honestly, this jackhammer was a welcomed improvement from the bombing exercises that had gone on yesterday morning.

"Hailey!" Her mother barged into the bedroom and stood with her arms folded. "You've been up here for a day, girl, it's time to get your act together."

"I know, Mama." She answered with a groan and sat up, then rooted around for a couple aspirins in her bedside table.

"What happened at that party? Did you drink anything?"

She didn't remember much of what had happened on Saturday night, but it had sure been one helluva party. This was shaping up to be a memorable senior year. There was no way she'd miss any part of the last week of school, even if she had to down aspirins and fake it through the day.

"Of course not." She lied with a smile, but the guilt built inside her. Her mom and dad expected better of her. If they knew she'd had alcohol, they'd never let her leave the house again.

She was supposed to be the model daughter.

"Hmmm. Breakfast is downstairs. Hurry up and get ready for school, love."

Hailey nodded, popped a few tablets and ground them to bitter dust.

Beep, beep.

A notification sounded and she grasped her cell, then unlocked it.

Where are you?

It was a direct message tweet from Maria. That was weird. Maria never asked after her – they were besties, but Maria was too busy being popular to worry about her location.

On my way. :-)

Hailey tweeted back.

She chose her outfit carefully, pairing form-fitting blue jeans with a green top that accentuated her eyes. Her copper-colored hair framed her face in loose curls that rested on her shoulders, and she layered on cherry blossom pink lip gloss, which was her favorite because Gino Batalha had told her it made her lips look delicious.

She'd harbored a crush on him since middle school, but he'd never made a move and she'd been too shy to make a move herself. For six months during junior year she'd had to pretend she didn't care that he was dating her best friend Maria.

Half an hour later she was in her car on her way to school.

Leaving with a bang was a big thing for Hailey. This morning, she'd walk in, hook up with Maria and own the hallways.

A car horn blared and jolted Hailey out of her own head. She mashed her brakes and brought her runaway vehicle to a screeching halt.

The driver behind the wheel of the Volkswagen shook her fist and flashed a zap sign.

She'd veered onto the other side of the road and had almost driven into a car leaving the school compound. Her cheeks burned and her stomach twisted in anxious knots.

"Sorry, sorry!" She raised her hand and yelled the hurried apologies, then rushed into the parking lot before too many people noticed.

It was 10 minutes before nine, which was enough time to catch up with her friends before class. Hailey parked and slipped out of the car, slamming the door with her hip.

Several juniors – guys mostly – loitered nearby, acting 'cool' with glasses on in the morning light. They hadn't even gone to the party. She ignored them and made a stroll past, but soft snickers gave her pause.

Hailey glared back at them, but they didn't have any shame. That was weird. Whatever, they were just kids.

She made her way inside and strutted down the corridor that held the senior lockers.

A tall, slim guy walked past her in the opposite direction and eyed her from head to toe like a piece of meat at the butcher's. He'd been in her homeroom class for years and they'd never looked each other directly in the face. What the hell? She scowled back at him.

Two junior girls passed her, giggling and pointing. Hailey considered telling them off for whatever snide comments they'd made, and for being in the senior hall for that matter, but she pulled up short and frowned.

It wasn't just them: everybody in the hallway stared at her. A few pointed and others made poor attempts at faking disinterest.

"What the hell is going on? Am I being pranked?" she muttered. "Ha! Nice try seniors. You guys almost got me." She smiled her brightest at the gawkers and continued down the hall.

She stopped dead in her tracks a few feet of her locker. Her stomach lurched and it wasn't because of that wild party this time.

Dread and shame overwhelmed her.

A hand grabbed her shoulder and spun her around.

It was Maria – her best friend.

"Maybe next time you'll think twice before you make moves on what's mine, slut."

Hailey's back hit the lockers hard, then her feet slid out from beneath her. Maria hovered above, smirking. She showered a stack of papers on Hailey's head.

"I've taken the liberty of posting these all over the school, so everyone can see what a slut you are. And trust me, there's a whole lot more where these came from."

Hailey's hands shook. She held the pictures that were dumped in her lap, horror building within her.

They were from Saturday night and she didn't remember being with any of these guys.

"This can't be real." She sat on the floor, staring in shock at picture after picture of her nude and involved in an orgy with a bunch of men she didn't know.

A couple guys were from the school's football team, but she didn't even know the five other guys. In fact, she didn't recognize anything she saw going on in the photographs that had been dumped in her lap.

The pictures showed her in various sexual positions and being posed to perform sexual favors. The guys that didn't participate in the shot laughed, smiled, and in some cases egged on the proceedings.

There was one where she was clearly out of it mentally, and her best friend took a picture with the two of them.

Maria had Hailey's face positioned by her crotch while she stuck her tongue out for the camera. It was disgusting.

The muscles of her stomach clenched and she puked on the students to her left. It served them right for relishing in what had happened to her. Their cries of disgust were almost drowned out by the gleeful exclamations of other onlookers.

The commotion echoed in the hallways and her ears. Hailey didn't have to look up to know that this was filmed on multiple cell phones. There was sure to be a bunch of videos on YouTube, Instagram, Vine and Facebook within a few minutes.

Not to mention the number of tweets and status messages that must be updating this second.

She was on the verge of tears, but she fought it as hard as she could. She couldn't give them the satisfaction of seeing that weakness right now. The laughter and jeering of the others got rowdier by the second. Then someone got out of line and threw a book at her.

"Yow, what the hell was that? This ain't funny. Stop."

The hall erupted in laughter at her weak attempt to stand up for herself. Guess there was nothing about a girl splayed out on the floor surrounded by vomit that would invoke people to take her seriously.

Please, let the Earth open up and swallow her now.

No one felt sorry about her predicament. No one thought that those pictures showed a girl being taken advantage of and violated. For the first time she felt the effects of bullying.

This kind of thing was never supposed to happen to someone like her. She wasn't the pinnacle of things, but she and Maria had been best friends since they were little.

Maria was head cheerleader, homecoming queen and she only dated older guys and top athletes.

Hailey always rode her social wave and enjoyed the kick back from being associated with the cool kids without catching the hatred from actually rolling with them.

If you really looked at things, then Hailey was actually a nerd. She studied computer science and spent most of her weekends online, playing games or studying. She would've been an easy target for the eagle-eyed bullies if it wasn't for Maria.

"Ho!" A junior yelled in the crowd.

"What a slut. Wow." Another of her friends remarked to Maria.

"I know, right? She loved every minute of it. She couldn't get enough."

Gino stood nearby, shaking his head, staring as if he'd never seen her before.

Pain speared her.

"I didn't enjoy it. I didn't even know it was happening. Can't you see?" Hailey pleaded, but Gino turned and pushed his way out of the milling students. Her words had fallen on deaf ears.

This was all she had coming. Hailey used the sleeve of her shirt to wipe the vomit from her mouth. Maria's brown, knee-high boots were still positioned in front of her. Hailey tried to steady herself and stuck her hand in vomit instead. Tears welled up.

"What did I do to deserve this? I thought you were my friend."

Maria scowled at her.

"Aw, poor Chiquita," she said, and pouted her full red lips in feigned sympathy. "Don't pretend to be the victim now, you little slut."

Maria crouched down until they were almost face to face. Maria's long dark hair hung in a braid over one shoulder. The silver friendship chain and pendant Hailey had given her when they were little girls and lived next door to each other hung around her neck.

She hissed into Hailey's ear. "Gino is mine and don't you ever forget it."

Hailey sat still as the girl she'd called her best friend got up and morphed into the mob crowding around her. Two teachers and the janitor pushed their way through to her, yelling at some of the kids.

Hailey had to get away. She had to get out and home before her parents found out. Before the entire world found out.

She gasped for air and her vision went speckled with grey.

Then her head hit the floor with a thud and the lights went out.

The Corporate Lawyer

Corporate lawyers were a dime a dozen in the concrete jungle.

"So, CialCorp. That's made your day, hasn't it?" Jerry, the mailman, slipped a few envelopes onto his desk.

"More like it's made my career," Billy Whitland replied. Why they even had mailmen these days was beyond him. That was what email was for. Billy shook his head and dismissed the guy with a wave, but the mailman didn't meander off to whatever hole he'd appeared out of straight away. "Thanks, Jeremy. See you around."

"It's Jerry." The guy paused and raised both eyebrows. Jerry, Jeremy, whatever. It didn't make a difference to Billy. What was this guy's deal? He didn't have time to mince words with the lesser mortals at the firm.

Billy gestured again, another wave of dismissal, but the mailman didn't budge.

He narrowed his eyes, flopped wayward and asked,

"What's it like?"

"What's what like?" Billy picked the mail up and tapped one of the long white envelopes on the corner of his desk. It was likely junk mail or a bill. Hardly anyone used snail mail anyway.

"Being up here, being the big man in the big office, you know?" Jerry folded his arms.

"Look, ah, Jeremy," Billy said, but the guy let out a small exclamation and he paused.

"It's Jerry. Damn, it's not that hard of a name to remember, but

I suppose I should expect nothing less from you."

"Huh?" Billy wasn't often stumped when it came to words, but this guy's behavior was outlandish.

"Yeah, you're above me, right? You're a big shot lawyer and I'm just the guy who brings your bills."

Billy drummed his knuckles on the desk and studied his laptop screen. There was too much to do. He had a meeting soon. He shrugged his watch down his arm and checked the time.

"You're absolutely right, Jeremy." Billy answered, though he knew what the guy's name was by now. "I am above you. I am more important. I have a more important job. Now, I suggest you get the hell out of my office before I have security remove you."

Jerry glared at him for a moment, mouth moving soundlessly. Billy ignored him and returned his attention to his screen.

The door snapped shut behind him, and he let out a long, low sigh.

It wasn't easy to get ahead in this business. Hell, it wasn't easy to be successful at all.

William Whitland had spent many years as a struggling young lawyer before he made it into a major firm. Now was his time: he was poised to make his name in the legal arena.

CialCorp was a hot technology company that'd dominated its space in the market for a number of years.

"Big Data," he whispered the word with reverence.

The company could collect private information about its clients and use it for marketing, development, just about anything else. It'd be unbeatable. Thus, its IPO would be the biggest event on the stock market for the year.

This assignment had landed on his plate and overseeing its success would finally gain him respect with the partners of the Cunningham and Wilson Law Office.

It was his ticket to the big time.

And with a big client like CialCorp in his portfolio he'd have enough clout to gain entry into the exclusive Leather Lounge. It was the premiere club where the finest lawyers and judges in the city met and socialized.

Many high-profile cases had been debated in the cushioned armchairs of the club among the cigar smoke and finely aged liquor. Or so the rumors said.

Billy pounded his large fists on his desk in frustration. He'd dedicated his life to this practice, and maintained a formidable success rate, only for his boss, Joseph Fitzgerald, to claim the big wins as his own. Fifteen years was enough sucking the hind teat.

His nails dug into his palms, biting into his flesh, and the pain brought him out of his mental preamble. Billy ran his hand along the smooth finish of his hardwood desk. He'd always liked to feel the coolness against his skin and it helped soothe the stinging in his palms.

He grabbed the phone on the corner of his desk and pressed a button. "Lorraine, please hold any calls for me. Tell anyone who calls that I'm busy."

Billy disconnected the line to his secretary and walked over to the glass windows of his office.

He resented not getting enough credit for his efforts at the practice, but having this office had been satisfactory consolation ... for a while.

These were his four walls. His privacy was secure, and he had a massive window to the outside, and good furniture was a major step up from a rickety desk on an open floor. But the novelty had definitely worn off after eight years in the same position.

The weather changed quickly, Billy noticed. After lunch the sun had shone and the weather had been warm enough that he'd removed the jacket of his gray suit and cranked up the a/c in his office. It was less than an hour later, and the dark clouds rolled in from the east.

He had two meetings as well as a court appearance scheduled for the day, and commuting all over town in heavy rain would be a pain in his rear end. His watch alarm beeped; he had half an hour to get out of the office and make it to court. Time had gotten away from him. He stuffed his mail in his briefcase for perusal later on and focused on addressing important emails.

But his inbox overflowed with spam instead – some were inappropriate ads for certain "enlargements" and his face flushed. He clicked to close and unsubscribe those emails unaware that, by the action of clicking, he was giving permission to some background programs to run on his computer.

"Spam mail? Hmm. Better report that to IT tomorrow."

Billy sent an email to Mr. Nick Neveu, the CFO of CialCorp, with invoices for his legal services as their primary advisor on the upcoming IPO, then shut down his system and rushed out the door.

It had been a long morning of meeting and hobnobbing with pretentious businessmen and their cronies. He just wanted to finish up in court and get back to the office before the day ended.

He had a massive company to manage.

"I think we can consider this meeting a success." Geoff Westhouse, one of the most powerful businessmen along the East Coast, rapped his knuckles on the desk.

His money was protected behind a legal arsenal that would have made the entire Persian army flinch.

"I'm glad we could come to an agreement," Billy said.

"I can't thank you enough," Geoff grinned, presenting whitened teeth to the room of his business partners and Billy. "This will provide the company and my son with a better future."

Billy steeled himself to ask the question that was expected. "And how is your boy?" This was the part which ate at him: pretending he gave a damn about their lives.

He wasn't cut out for this. He was supposed to be in charge!

The guy at the top controlling things, not the little man on the floor schmoozing the clients and licking boot.

"He's doing fantastic. Attending Harvard of course. Where else?"

"A fitting university for a Westhouse," Billy answered with an obsequious nod. Hopefully that'd be the end of it.

His boss was exactly like these people. His boss was the kind of guy who would shove a knife in your back whilst hugging you and whispering in your ear that it was acupuncture.

There was only so much a guy could take of that before retreating to his dungeon of solitude became a welcomed idea.

"I'll see you again next Tuesday." He shook hands with Westhouse and the rest of the partners then saw them to the elevator.

The ride down was filled with awkward silences and attempts at cute conversation.

He exited the elevator and made a quick beeline for his office. He was careful not to make eye contact with any of the plebeians in the bullpen nor glance into any of the offices along the corridor. Not even the ever-faithful Lorraine got much more than an obligatory wave as he disappeared into his office.

Billy closed the door behind him.

Ring.

"Can't a guy just catch a break?" He sighed and dragged himself over to his desk. "If this isn't anyone important then God knows they'll get voicemail." The caller ID said it was the IT department.

The call made him raise an eyebrow. This is new. "Hello, William Whitland speaking."

"Hi Mr. Whitland, This is Jonah from IT. We just wanted to speak with you regarding some complaints of unwanted mail being sent from your email address. This is an official notice to cease and desist if you are sending them purposely. However, if you are having a problem, Mr. Whitland, then now would be the time to report it."

This was unbelievable.

He stood in front of his desk staring at the receiver.

The little prick Jonah had hardly been with the company for a good two months and for some reason felt he could talk to him this way?

There was nothing he could say which was appropriate for the workplace, so he gently placed the receiver on the cradle.

He'd hardly been in his office for days. Anyone who thought he had time to spam them was ridiculous.

Little droplets of sweat formed on his forehead and a single bead trickled down his back.

It was about 82 degrees Fahrenheit outside. Summer was nearly in full swing and Billy was already miserable. Between work and the business meals, keeping fit had been pushed to the bottom of the list.

He wasn't fat, but he did have a little more weight than he should in the arms and the mid-section. The extra padding made him sweat more during the summer, so for about three months he had to practically live in air-conditioning to avoid walking around like a pig ready for roasting.

He turned on the air conditioner and hovered in front of it. The cool air blew on his face, allowing him a few lucid thoughts.

There had to be some merit to the claims for him to get called about it. It wasn't like he was one of the juniors in the bullpen: he wouldn't be 'cold-called' about it unless the emails were especially bothersome.

He sat down in his plush, brushed leather chair and started up the PC. He had a ton of unread mail in his inbox to clear. Some were status updates from clients for matters that had already been addressed. He made sure to skim through and delete those messages.

There were at least eight emails from co-workers asking him to desist from sending them subscription invitations. Apparently his account had been used to send marketing notices for all kinds of things ranging from Canadian online pharmacies offering great deals on Viagra to coupon offers for stationery.

His eyes widened and his pulse beat a tattoo against his neck. Although most of them had been sent internally he noticed that amidst the jumble of generic spam there'd been an email sent to the CFO of CialCorp, Nick Neveu, just today.

"Good God, if there is a God, I hope this shit doesn't screw up my plans. I don't deserve this shit." Billy buried his head in his hands.

His secretary suddenly appeared by the door. "Excuse me sir, Mr. –"

"What is it now Lorraine?!"

His tone took her aback and she stood flabbergasted for a second. But she regained that cool composure quicker than a bullet left a gun. It was why he kept her around even though she was well past retirement age.

The woman knew how to brush things aside and keep things professional and progressive. He'd make it up to her sometime.

"Mr. Neveu is on line one for you, Mr. Whitland."

"Thank you very much, Lori." It was his pet name for her and she knew it was his way of saying he was sorry without actually having to say it. She smiled subtly in response. "Please take a message for any other calls. I will be going back out for lunch after this meeting."

"No problem, Mr. Whitland." She gave him a stiff nod and closed the door.

Billy sat for a moment with his eyes clenched shut, slowly sucking air into his lungs and releasing it slowly through his mouth. It was a calming exercise he'd learned from his second wife who had been a meditation instructor.

Sometimes he regretted their break up but the phenomenal sex didn't counter the woman's lack of intelligence. Thank God they'd never had kids.

At least the meditation came in handy. It was important in the legal profession to hide the fleshy underbelly of anxiety regardless of the circumstance. Anything else and it would all come crashing down. He took another breath.

"Hello, Billy Whitland here. How can I help you today, Mr. Neveu?" He put on the cheeriest voice he could manage. His plan was to get the CFO on his back foot and railroad the entire situation to come out looking squeaky clean and in control.

"Um, Mr. Whitland I'm calling regarding a puzzling email I received from you. With our IPO just around the corner we cannot afford to have certain matters made public knowledge before all regulatory measures and proprietary content have been properly implemented and secured."

"Mr. Neveu, I assure you that there is no need to worry on my end, but the small matter of a little virus in the company software; just typical stuff though. The IT department is scrubbing the servers as we speak."

"A virus? Mr. Whitland, I'm referring to correspondence received today. It included an invoice attachment with a breakdown of some of the work you've been handling for us over the past two months." Neveu cleared his throat before continuing, "I was concerned because we had settled this matter only last week and had agreed from the beginning that any details regarding our company would be handled via paper correspondence or in person." He waited for an answer.

Billy struggled to find the words and Neveu took the opportunity to continue, "I certainly hope I do not need to fear for our company's financial security, Mr. Whitland. Security is of the highest importance with us and I expect that as a consultant for the company, you would be holding yourself to the same standards. Otherwise I may be forced to terminate this contract."

The conversation had taken an unexpected turn. Billy was prepared to talk about some spam emails, but this was serious. It was clear someone had tried to set him up and discredit him. It had to be a competitor from another firm who'd decided to play dirty and take part in some corporate sabotage.

His ears grew warm and the familiar stinging pain in his palms accompanied the heat. It had been a long, hard 15 years. There was no way he'd let it go down the drain like this.

"Mr. Neveu, I apologize for the email. I believe my secretary must have gotten her wires crossed. Trust me. I will take care of this, right now. I assure you that you have nothing to worry about."

It took a few more minutes of calm assurance to satisfy Mr. Neveu before he could finally end the call. Billy fumed in his office chair, swivelling from side to side. He had to get to the bottom of the situation.

He reported the issue with his email address to IT via email. He refused to give Jonah the satisfaction of calling back. He packed up his things and headed out to a late lunch. Billy exited his office and locked the door behind him.

"Have there been any more calls for me, Lorraine?"

"No sir." She glanced up from organizing files on her desk.

"Lorraine, you're fired. Clean out your desk immediately and report to HR for your severance."

Billy marched off without another word. He had to figure out where the spam was coming from and who had compromised his company email. It couldn't really have been her, but he couldn't afford doubts. He had to cover all his bases.

And that meant getting hold of an old friend.

The College Graduate

"You're Jia, right?" He shuffled into her office wearing the jeans and loose Van Halen shirt he thought were super cool. Apparently.

What a loser.

"I think you know that by now, Greg." He was the other intern, the one in competition with her for the position. Not that he could be labelled real 'competition'. He was useless at his job, that much was clear.

"Yeah, I just wanted to chat with you about some of the requests we've been getting around here." Greg shuffled forward, his ginger hair catching the daylight streaming through her office window.

He was kind of attractive in a weird way. A part from the whole Van Halen thing - gross.

"What about them?" They hadn't handled anything too strange

in IT, and certainly nothing she couldn't handle with her background.

"They just seem a little intense, don't you think?"

Greg chewed his bottom lip and pressed his hands together.

"Intense," Jia repeated with a flicker of a smile. This guy was toast. There was simply no way he'd ever beat her out of Paradigm.

This job was as good as hers.

"Look, Greg, if you need help with something, spit it out. I don't mind."

"That would be highly unethical," he snapped back, showing a bit of fire and she pulled a face.

"All right, then I don't see how I can help you, or what you're doing in my office." Jeez, she was all for helping someone else out, but why bite the hand that feeds you.

Greg stared at her for several moments, studying her face intently. There was a keen light in his eyes she'd never noticed before, more intelligence than he normally gave off. It disconcerted her and she shrugged her shoulders.

"Is there something else I can help you with?" She pressed her lips together and frowned slightly.

"No. Not yet." Greg gave a cursory nod then loped out of her office.

That was weird. Jia shook her long dark hair back and cleared her mind. There was the matter at hand to attend to.

She cleaned her desk with meticulous precision, stomach bubbling with anticipation.

Her plans moved ahead swimmingly. The game-plan had probably been set from birth, but certainly from the moment her parents decided to send her to America to live with her aunt at 14.

The culture shock had been jarring. She'd received strict schooling in China. The focus on academics and being the best was first and foremost on every student's mind. But in America, there was a strange obsession with looks and social standing that Jia didn't get.

Many days she'd asked herself what make-up, sex and celebrity gossip would do for these young people in the future and couldn't come up with an answer.

Of course, that meant she'd pretty much been a social outcast. Thankfully she'd been considered exotically pretty, which had spared her the experience of being bullied.

She'd managed to stay focused, survive high school and graduate as valedictorian with the support of her emigrated family. The day she'd given her parents the news they'd celebrated with the entire community, which had banded together to send her gifts and good-fortune talismans from back home.

Jia came from a small, rural farming community in Northern China, so her success was a hero story for those back home. The scholarship she won helped to fuel the dream of two rice farmers for their only daughter to do more than menial labor for the rest of her life.

Her time at university was no cake walk. It had been a grueling process. It took many sleepless nights, personal sacrifices and a few mornings of shame, but she'd graduated on time and in the top of her class with a First Class degree in Computer Science and Law. Now, she was on her probation period at an exceptional investment firm.

Her three-month period was just about over. Jia had been vigilant about presenting herself as an asset and being efficient in her work. The firm had taken in five interns, but only intended to keep three when the probation time was up.

There were two interns in the IT department and it was pretty obvious that one of them would be cut. Jia wasn't too perturbed though. The intern she competed with was always slower than her in finishing his assigned tasks, and it was obvious he struggled to accomplish things she found rudimentary.

Securing this job was a social game, so she made sure to play the field. If the supervisor wanted coffee then he got it. If one of the senior executives needed paperwork rushed over to "Bob" then "Bob" would receive those documents with a smile.

This job was hers.

She'd even written to her parents about it. All she waited on was the official papers to sign. She was lost in her thoughts and anxiety, tapping her feet under her desk.

"Ugh!" She grunted in exasperation. "Just a few more days and I'll be solid."

Ring. It was her phone.

"Hello, this is Jia Kailai. Junior IT intern. How can I help?"

"Jia, this is Jeff. Umm. There's no easy way to say this, but the company has decided not to keep you. Your actions have been against the company policy about diplomacy and discretion for our clients. Please pack your things immediately. Security will escort you out."

Click. He hung up.

The line was dead. Jia sat in shock.

She struggled to lift the last box representing her life at Paradigm Enterprises Inc. into her lime green Ford Fiesta. The lost opportunity made her eyes prickle and water.

What the hell had been the point of all the hard work and long hours? She was still in the parking garage with the slacker who'd been an intern in the marketing department just so he would actually have something on his résumé before he took up a head executive position at his rich father's company.

She stared at him climbing into a sleek, silver BMW sports car without a care in the world and it made her feel sick. His nonchalance infuriated her. He'd received his end of internship papers with a smile and rode down in the elevator beside her.

He revved up the engine of his car and cruised by her on his way out. He tipped his shades downward and eyed her with the subtlety of a pack of hyenas stalking dying prey. Not that she was easily shocked, or didn't know how to appreciate male attention, but there was little pleasure in the crass manner in which he looked her up and down licking his lips.

"Hey. Seen you around the office. Why don't you hop that tight ass in the passenger seat and let me take you for a ride?"

His eyes never left her hips.

Her skirt wasn't tight, nor was Jia particularly shapely, but the gym had given her a slender toned body with some nice curves. Usually she was very confident and upfront when it came to relations with the opposite sex, but this guy made the hair on the nape of her neck stand on end.

His name was Brian Denbow. He was the son of entertainment mogul Sean Denbow and heir to a mass media marketing throne. If he'd had to work for anything money could buy, Jia would've eaten her stapler.

"I'd rather get hit by a comet." It popped out before she could stop it. Maybe it was the bitterness over being fired from a job she was absolutely perfect for.

Had Greg sabotaged her?

He'd been in her office.

"Aw, come on baby, let's go for a ride."

Her face reflected her disgust but Brian was unfazed. He merely chuckled, rolled up his heavily tinted window and sped off, leaving Jia alone with her thoughts.

People like that under-qualified and classless prick of a person got by easily in life by getting a hand up, while she missed out on her dreams even though she'd put her all in to attain them.

She'd done whatever they'd wanted. She'd worked harder than most CEOs, she was sure of it. And this was her grand reward.

She gestured to the underground parking lot and let out a half-sob, half-chuckle. It was a candid mix of hysteria. She had worked so hard.

The tears warmed her cheeks. Her knees went weak. She was tired of the world and its corrupt policies. Jia made her way to her car and climbed into her passenger seat. She curled into a ball and cried so hard that her tan slacks were soaked with a mixture of snot and tears.

Eventually she sat up and wiped her cheeks. It was about 3:30 p.m. If she didn't leave now then he'd have witnesses to her breakdown. Jia climbed over into the driver's seat and started up the engine. Driving out of the parking lot for the last time depressed her.

The moment she exited the parking lot she'd begin a period of sheer uncertainty in her life. There had been no contingency plan to the firm and now she had to face the world without her armor of confidence.

She sighed heavily and rested her forehead on the steering wheel.

"This is stupid," she whispered it to herself. "There are other firms in the country, and with credentials like mine, there is no way that finding another job would be difficult."

The little pep talk made her roll her eyes at herself. The job market was pretty shitty. There were a ton of graduates knocking about so the process of getting a new job wouldn't be all sunshine and rainbows. In any case, she'd take the afternoon off from worrying about it.

"Screw this place!" she yelled it for release. "Screw my supervisor, and screw you Jeff Aceves! Time to get out of here." She eyed her phone on the passenger seat. Jia picked it up, took a selfie and then a picture of the boxed belongings in the back seat. Then she posted a composite picture on Instagram.

Last day at work. Totally sucks. These guys are dicks! #fired #outta-here but first … #lemmetakeaselfie

The Disgruntled Employee

Greg Davoli hated being undercover.

"Did you hear? Jia got the boot."

Obviously he'd heard, he'd been her competition in the IT department, but whatever brain fart had seen her fired, had gotten him promoted.

"Yeah, I heard." Greg nodded to his co-worker and buried himself in his computer again. He hated being interrupted.

"You must be pretty darn excited," Jones continued, twiddling his pen between his fingers. He held it up and moved it so fast it looked as if the pen had bent in the middle.

"Yeah, I'm over the moon," Greg replied in a monotone.

Jones ruffled his spiked-up hair and gave him a side glance. "You should be man, but don't let it go to your head."

"Huh?" What didn't this guy understand? He had more important things to do than talk to him. Greg tapped his fingers on the keys and pretended to pick up work again, but Jones didn't excuse himself.

"They only hired you because Jia made some big mistake. It's the talk of the office, man. I'm surprised you didn't hear about it."

"What mistake?"

"I don't know, something to do with flash drives or something. Who cares?" Jones popped a piece of Nicorette chewing gum between his two front teeth and crunched down hard. "Point is, they would've hired her if she didn't make some big mistake."

Greg studied the obnoxious man for a moment then gave the slow smile he'd learned as a kid. It was totally ironic and devoid of pleasure. He arched one eyebrow slightly.

The gormless pencil pusher got the point and wandered off.

Jia had been a hard worker, played the social game flawlessly, had been young and set for success. He hated that he'd stolen the position from her, but what choice did he have?

This was his job. Get in, get the information, make the arrest.

Greg considered the computer and planned his next move. He might have the opportunity to do some real undercover snooping now that Mr. 'Big Shot' Aceves was in a meeting.

Greg had been invited to join the FBI seven years ago, even though at the time he'd been pretty much a rookie cop. In less than a year, Greg had made more successful arrests than any other agent in his division, and closed more cases than any other FBI rookie.

That record had set him up as a big target for spite and jealousy among the veteran agents. He was glad to be out from under the thumb of mediocrity and complacency.

The agency had quickly recognized that Greg had more potential than a field agent, so after three months on the beat, he'd been called back to headquarters for training as an undercover agent.

Greg had youthful features, which allowed him to pass for either a college student or a recent graduate with ease. He usually kept a small goatee and a neat buzz cut which suited his chiseled facial structure, but his handlers made him change his look to a much longer hipster beard and wear his hair in a scruffy-looking ponytail.

He ruffled his hair. At least this job allowed him some leeway with the hair.

His father was ex-military, so he'd been trained from a young age that presentation said a lot about a man's character. This look made him feel like a hobo. That was the first strike against undercover work. Secondly, it was obvious that undercover work meant long periods away from his distant family – his nieces and nephews specifically. The separation burned him to the core every time he was called to action.

This particular run undercover was close to a strike three. The assignment was a drawn out exercise in zombie world survival. It killed him to show up for work everyday at this bureaucratic nightmare of a company and pretend he wasn't as knowledgeable as he was. But he was assigned to play out this young hippy role he'd been given.

Many days he'd sit at his desk and stare at the computer screen in the hope he'd seem so focused that no one would bother him with inconsequential office gossip. He didn't care about anything but completing his mission so he could get the hell out of Dodge.

He rubbed his hands together and gave a sigh. The end of the day couldn't come quickly enough.

The agency already knew that the infamous 'Gang of 8' had major ties with this company and the big heads were convinced they were hot on the trail of one of the eight bigwigs running the operation. But Greg wasn't quite convinced that any of these buffoons were capable of managing a crime syndicate, and if Aceves was part of the gang after all, he'd laugh himself silly.

The boss man was the biggest idiot of the lot and bringing him down would be a grand pleasure.

Something *was* up though, and there was more to it than phony investment schemes and money laundering.

There was a deep rot and he had to find a way to expose it and burn it from the face of the earth like the infection it was.

Ring.

The phone on his desk blared into action and he snatched up the receiver.

"Davoli speaking."

"Brother." There was a slight hiss of static and a click, " - had to call."

Greg took the receiver from his ear, shook his head once then replaced it.

"Hey, Sis, what's up?" Hearing from her was a pleasant surprise. It was another reason he hated his job: he was far from what little family he had.

If he had a choice, he wouldn't be here. He'd be back in Recife with them.

There were more crackles and pops and he pulled a face. Bad reception was one of his biggest pet peeves. "Can't quite make out what you said there, Sis. Can you repeat that please?"

"It's about Hailey."

His niece was the treasure of their family. She was set to head to college and generally kick butt until she made it big.

It was the opposite of what Greg had achieved in his life, and he couldn't be more proud. Hopefully she made wiser choices and didn't end up married to a job. The kid was the star and he loved hearing about her success.

Greg grinned and relaxed in the office chair. It creaked beneath his weight and he stretched his gangly legs in front of him.

"What about her?"

"Something terrible has happened." Her voice cracked, and it wasn't the connection which was the problem this time.

"What are you talking about?"

The line cleared up and a strangled sob came through, followed by a whispered oath.

"Spill the beans, Sis. You're starting to freak me out here." He hunched down and checked to make sure there was no one listening in. He hated making phone calls in public. Hell, he didn't even have a Facebook account – that's how private he was.

His sister, Rosemaire, cried into the phone for a good two minutes. "She went to a party on Friday and she was taken advantage of."

Greg grasped a pencil in his left hand and squeezed tight.

"Can you better define that for me?" It was FBI talk. It helped cut the anger back to a minimum.

"She went to a party and her friend drugged her and took naked pictures of her with men. Students mostly. Doing things. Sexual things." It came out in a stream and sputtered off into sobs at the end.

"No. This can't be." He refused it with a curt shake of his head.

"She's broken, Greg. She's putting on a brave face like she can make it through, but it's taking a toll on her each day. The kids are relentless, they won't leave her alone."

"What do you mean?"

"They've plastered the internet with the pictures. She's had to delete her Twitter, Facebook, Google plus, Flickr, Tumblr, I don't know, every account she's ever had. The only thing she has left is her blog."

This was why he didn't engage in the poisonous social media culture of this century. If there was any news, good or bad, it could be found there first. Murdered soldiers in Syria plastered alongside pictures of cats in funny hats.

It was sick. Nothing was sacred anymore. But there was nothing he could do to stem the tide of filth. And he couldn't leave the country in the middle of this case. If he lost a lead on the Gang of 8, it would be over for him.

"Rose, if I could get down there I would, but there are things here…" Davoli checked the coast again and scratched at his chest.

"I know, Bro. I just wanted you to know. I just wanted to hear the voice of sanity in all this. To know there are real people out there who care about what happens to us." Rose's tone hardened with the strength which was innate to their family. They'd had the same father - suffered through the same verbal abuse.

"The family or humanity in general? I'm beginning to have my doubts." He muttered it, but she gave a light sigh.

"I have to go."

Click. The line went dead and the dial tone sang in his ear. The whine matched the growing anger in the back of his mind.

This was what the world had perpetrated.

This take all, destroy and burn and steal. It drove him to distraction.

He hated this job, but he had to do it. To prevent things like this from happening, to add a little good where there was so much bad.

It was about 3:30 in the afternoon and Greg had the 'Midweek Blues', made worse by this *fantastic* news. The executives and supervisors were in a meeting so there'd be no harm in a little investigative snooping.

He hacked into the encrypted folders which were sent automatically when IT did maintenance. They were sent with discrete monitoring Trojans, which would scan emails and documents for specific keywords and later Greg could retrieve the information from them.

It was mind-boggling that this was the first time he was free of a micro-managing jerk of a boss to do something this simple.

An alert popped up on his computer. Greg's eyes opened wide and his jaw fell open. He couldn't believe this.

His fingers inched toward the keyboard.

"Yeah, yeah, Anand. Just do what you gotta do, okay? I've got some business to attend to." Jeff Aceves came strolling by and he minimized the browser window.

He had his usual blonde bimbo in tow – an assistant he'd hired for obvious reasons, and none of them had to do with clerical work. Conjugal was a more apt expression.

"Can I help you with anything, Boss?" Blondie cooed, practically clinging to his arm. He shrugged her off with a grin and glanced around the room, importantly.

Greg eyed him from beneath his brow, pretending an eagle-like focus on his screen.

Mr. Aceves was in the Gang of 8 after all.

"Yeah, get me a cappuccino with extra cream would ya?"

Jeff turned his attention on Greg, who made an appropriate flinch for a newbie college grad under the glare of a high-powered boss. Really, he wanted to slap this guy in cuffs and cart him off to HQ for questioning. Greg knew that Jeff's investment schemes were for laundering money from innocent pensioners. But there was another reason he was this smug of late. Greg wanted to know what was that reason.

"You're new." Jeff observed, while his assistant scurried off to order or make (probably milk the cows, too) the said cappuccino with extra cream. "I don't like newbies. Too soft." He studied his nails.

"Y-yeah, I'm n-new," Greg stammered in fake awe.

Jeff's ego was placated and he puffed his chest out like a parakeet. "Welcome aboard, kiddo. Make sure you don't mess up this opportunity."

"I won't, sir." He gritted his teeth, hopefully that made him sound nervous rather than incensed.

Aceves raised a pudgy finger, that cream had taken its toll, and waggled it. "You get one chance at this company. Never forget that."

Then he sauntered off, cool as could be with the attractive assistant snapping at his heels.

Money could buy anything. Except integrity and good character.

But why had they fired Jia?

It didn't make sense – he'd played his cards well since his arrival at the firm, and he'd made sure to keep his head low so he could get in, get what he needed and hopefully get dismissed.

That had backfired and it couldn't be a coincidence.

Either Jia Kailai was in on the Gang of 8, or she'd stumbled upon information which had put the company at risk.

They would've had to fire her before she could figure anything out.

Alternatively, they'd fired her because she'd already figured it out.

The hacking had confirmed that the bigwigs at HQ had been onto something. Now it was time to get down and dirty, busy with the field work.

And Jia was his only real lead.

Greg logged off the computer, pushed his chair back and left the office.

// //

The Grandma

It had been almost 15 years since her husband of 40 years had passed away, but her love for him had never wavered to this day.

Mary gazed at their wedding portrait, reminiscing on a lifetime of happiness and special moments that made their marriage memorable. There she was frozen in time with her head thrown backward, hair blowing in the breeze and a flowing white wedding dress. The only significant difference between the young, radiant woman captured laughing while hand in hand with her newlywed husband and the finely aged lady today, was a reinforced foundation of that love with the passage of time.

Mary had met Leonard while working part-time as a cook in a diner. He'd dated a beautiful redheaded waitress at the time and he used to show up 10 minutes before closing time every night and wait to take her home.

Sometimes, while the waitress worked her tables, he'd call through the order window and make conversation with her about news, local politics, the weather or with some story he had from work.

They'd chatted easily and Mary was polite because he seemed like a nice guy. The waitress had been jealous and picked a fight, but that hadn't ended well. Next thing, Leonard was coming to the diner to see her and the pretty waitress was out of the picture.

The rest was love and bliss.

Although Mary had catered for parties and events on occasion, Leonard had been a fairly well-off businessman and had taken care of the family financially for their entire married life.

When he'd become sick and passed away, Mary had found out that he'd planned for that and had set up excellent health and life insurance plans.

In her golden years, Mary was able to live comfortably on the money and assets he'd left for her. She traced her husband's happy face with her finger. Her emerald engagement ring glinted in the sunlight and she couldn't help but smile. A small chuckle escaped her as she recalled betting Lenny that she'd be the one to reach 80 years old with all her teeth.

"Guess I win the bet, huh Len." A tear clung to her lashes. She had these bittersweet moments several times a week.

She kept the photo inside a gilded frame on the large oak desk Lenny had given her for their 20th wedding anniversary to symbolize the eternity of their love.

The only thing that shared the space with that photo was the laptop her daughter-in-law got her for Christmas a couple years ago. Old memories and that laptop were the only two things which kept her company on most days. Most of her friends had long passed and her only son lived with his family many miles away.

Mary kissed the photo of her dearly beloved husband and placed it back in its place of honor at her left hand on the desk.

She'd finished cleaning the house about an hour ago and had a casserole baking in the oven for a late lunch. She decided to kill some time with her favorite pastime: Facebook. There were so many interesting blogs and posts on the site that she could spend an entire day reading and watching videos.

Her favorites were those about food and inspirational quotes, especially when there were videos posted. Every time she watched a video it was like being away from home having a conversation with a new friend. Her son's wife showed her how to share the videos and posts that she liked with the family and the rest of her Facebook friends.

Today, there were three new videos among the picture posts. Mary watched a review about a guy's first attempt at double chocolate cake, then a young lady's advice on the best way to make a Swiss roll. Oh! She had a casserole in the oven, she'd nearly forgotten.

She quickly clicked the video to pause it and ran into the kitchen to save her lunch. She came back, but she'd shared the video instead of pausing it. The phone rang.

"Guess it doesn't matter. I'll just watch it later." She clicked the 'ok' button and went to phone.

"Hello! You've got Mary."

"Mrs. Dorowski, this is Edward Manning from the bank. There may be a problem with your account. Can I ask you a few questions?"

She'd loved Eddie because he was a cheerful guy, but this conversation chilled Mary to her core. Her entire world had just shifted and everything was about to crash and burn.

"What kind of questions? What's going on?"

"Your account has a deficit, Ma'am."

That was simply impossible. Len had handled the finances and she hadn't spent a cent more than she should have.

"What do you mean?"

"I think it would be better if you came down to the bank and discussed this with us. Shall we make an appointment for tomorrow morning?"

"I – I guess that would be all right. How is this possible, Eddie?"

The man softened and lowered his voice. "It's something to do with your investments, Mary. We need to talk about this in person. Does 9 a.m. suit you?"

Mary swivelled her head from side-to-side in disbelief.

"Yes, yes that should be fine. I'll see you then."

The line went dead.

Mary fumbled over to the computer and exited her Facebook

page. She opened her online banking profile instead and typed in her password: the day she'd married Len.

Error. Incorrect password. You will have three more attempts, after which you will be shut out from your account.

Mary breathed deep and tried again, her fingers shaking on the keys. She typed one letter per second, just to be sure she'd done it right this time.

Error. Incorrect password. You will have two more attempts, after which you will be shut out from your account.

"No, this can't be happening!" Mary opened the desk drawer beside her and brought out her 'financial file'. The legacy Len had left her.

"Always organize your papers, Mary love, otherwise you'll regret it." That was what he'd told her each time she'd complained about having to keep the clunky thing around.

"Guess you were right, Len." She offered silent thanks as well, then rifled through the papers and plastic sleeves.

Bank slips, budgets, bank reports and account details.

There! Her password. She'd gotten one of the letters wrong.

Mary steeled herself for the worst and typed the password in again.

The page refreshed and skipped through to her account and she breathed relief in a stream of air.

"Thank goodne –" The words faltered on her lips.

Her account wasn't empty, it was in the red.

"That can't be right. This is a nightmare." She muttered the words, clicking haplessly on the page. But no amount of fiddling would change what it said.

She was over $10,000.00 in overdraft.

It was impossible. She'd never owed or spent that much money in her entire life, let alone the past week.

The phone rang and she jumped, then patted her hair.

"Calm down, Mary," she told herself, "we'll get this sorted out."

She reached over and answered the phone for a second time that evening.

"Hello?" An ominous buzz answered her. "Hello? Who is this?"

"Aun – ?" The line was terrible, but the voice on the other end was male. The fear settled in behind Mary's eyes, and she rubbed at them with one hand.

"Who is this?" Mary asked, quivering from head to toe and staring at the desk.

"Auntie, it's Taylor." The line cleared up miraculously and she let out a soft sigh.

This was a pleasant surprise. She hadn't heard from her nephew since he'd moved to Texas with his wife and little girl.

"Taylor, love, it's been years. How are you?" The call couldn't have come at a better time. It was the perfect distraction, a good way to remind herself that there was happiness left. "How are Shannon and Deb?"

Taylor cut across her questions. "I'm not so good, Auntie Mary."

"Oh no, what's the matter?" She didn't need more bad news. Len had been the rock of the family, she wasn't great with managing crises in the family.

"I'm in a lot of trouble and I need help." Taylor was breathless, he was panicked and it set her already raw nerves jangling, wind chimes in the trees. "I need money."

"Oh gosh, Taylor, I don't think I can help you."

"Please, I have no one else to turn to." The line crackled and Taylor's voice distorted. "Please, you have to wire it to me."

The pop, pop of crackers in the background disturbed their conversation.

"I have to go Auntie, but please say, 'yes.' I can't get out of here without that money. You have to help me, please," he pleaded and her throat closed tight.

"I'm sorry, Tay, I don't have the money. I just don't have the money." Tears sprang up in her eyes and she scrunched them shut, but the drops fell over the rim of her lids and dripped to the desk.

"Plea –" Firecrackers exploded on the other end of the line, and it cut off seconds later.

Mary sat down in her chair, the phone dropping from her hand to the floor.

It struck her like a hammer between the eyes.

Those weren't crackers. They were gunshots.

CHAPTER 3

"You realize how important this is." Jeff paced back and forth in front of him, holding his hands behind his back and wearing a grimace like a superhero cape.

It was his magical defense against the reality of the Gang of 8.

"If you can't get this information before CialCorp goes live with the IPO," Aceves paused and scratched the back of his neck, "then –"

"Yeah, yeah, then everything fails. You can't take over the world or whatever." Anand grinned over the edge of his PC.

The grin was a total fake out. Jeff Aceves was a weak man and an irritation, a reminder of the fat underbelly of the west.

Capitalism, greed, dishonor.

"Don't give me cheek, buddy, I can't take it from you today." The 'boss man' rubbed at his temples and plopped down in the leather swivel chair facing Anand's desk.

"What's the matter?"

"Had a meeting with the other misters."

"Ah," Anand remarked, then returned to his screen without another comment. Jeff was Mr. 8, the least influential of the entire group … a noob, basically. Still, it worked in Anand's favor. The man was desperate for recognition from the rest of the criminal gang and that made him easier to prod in the right directions.

When the topic came up, Anand was instantly AFK in his mind.

"Tell me it'll work."

"What will?" He relished pissing off Jeff.

"You know exactly what I'm talking about," Aceves growled, pointing his dirty index finger at the hacker. "Don't mess around, Anand, I do NOT have the patience today."

He chuckled under his breath and shifted his glasses up his nose. "You need to relax. Of course it will work." Had he become this weak since he'd moved to the country? Jeff Aceves was a wreck. He had a real concept of risk, but no real backbone, and that would be his downfall.

"What have you got so far?" Jeff asked.

"Incredible skills. I'm the real one-three-three-seven."

"Pardon me?"

"Leet." Anand's half-smile was a strange movement for him. He didn't do 'cool' very well.

"I have no idea what you're talking about."

"It's techie talk for elite. It means I have mad skills."

"Can you just be serious for five damn seconds?" Jeff slammed the desk with a fist and Anand gave him a withering look.

"I'm targeting the CFO of CialCorp."

"And?" Jeff folded his arms, then let them loose again and swung them at his sides. He resumed the pacing, that incessant pacing, which would give Anand a headache in a second.

"And it's going well. I've got an 'in'. A lawyer working exclusively with the documentation for the upcoming IPO."

Jeff nodded and breathed through his mouth. It reminded Anand of a winded rhinoceros.

"That's fantastic news. Have you got it yet?"

"It's a little more complex than that. I've got access to his email account and sent out my custom exploits. They got in and are going through the company's network via spam mail. My little minions are hard at work with my sequence of commands. It's so simple, yet so effective."

"It's not too simple?"

"No such thing as too simple."

"The creator of the Club Sandwich would disagree."

The balding Mr. 8 jumped to his feet again and went over to the coffeemaker in the corner. Being relatively high up in the illegal gang had its positives: fresh coffee, a big office, and access to the information Anand needed to complete his mission.

Allahu Akbar.

"But I don't get it. Why don't you just target the CFO directly? He'll have all the information we need."

Anand rolled his eyes while Jeff's back was turned.

"Because that would leave a pretty obvious motive for anyone looking into our activity."

"Who's looking into our activity?" Jeff flinched, spilling coffee from the pot onto the lush carpet below.

"No one. But it's better to be safe than sorry." He'd never encountered such a taxing man in his entire life – and he was from the Middle East. "This is going to go down smoothly. Know why? Because I'm in charge of this. I'm doing everything to ensure we don't land on the wrong side of the law." Anand paused, then laughed again. "That's not right. We're already on the wrong side of the law, but I'm the one making sure we don't get caught."

"I don't know about this."

Anand was used to the conversation. It took place each day at the same time in his office. Jeff Aceves was terrified of discovery.

If they managed to take down CialCorp, it would make Jeff a very rich man, or so he thought. In reality, it would destroy his life, simply because Anand had a different motive.

He typed a few words into an email and shot it off back home.

"I still don't know if CialCorp is the best idea. There must be another way." Jeff lifted the cup to his lips and took a sip. "This is big. If the other misters find out about this …"

"Do you want to advance in the ranks? Do you want to prove yourself to those old dudes running the show?"

Jeff clutched the coffee cup and glared into space. "I want to be in charge."

"Then this is the only way."

CialCorp's IPO was a hot topic. Jeff believed having it meant insider trading, earning more money, proving himself to the bigwigs in the Gang of 8. He wanted to be Mr. 5 at least. Such grand ambitions for a pencil-pushing schemer.

But Jeff had no real concept of what CialCorp stood for.

He was a great businessman, sure, but social media, technological advancements and IT were beyond him.

That was Anand's specialization. The minute he'd happened upon CialCorp, sparks had gone off in his brain.

This company was unbelievable. Their algorithm for collecting public and private data from their customers made Google bots look like the fat kid at a track meet day.

Every tablet, computer, TV or smartphone manufactured in China had the algorithm embedded on the hardware itself. The minute a user signed in or started it up was the minute the collection started, regardless of the operating system used.

Location, shopping preference, eye color, height, favorite music, personal profile, it was all collected and stored away for future use. A company with that kind of information was unstoppable in the consumer market.

An individual with that information was unstoppable in many, many ways.

And a state?

Anand's slow smile made Jeff sit upright in the chair.

"What is it?"

"Just thinking of how rich we'll be," he lied, and Jeff's expression lit up significantly.

Greed. Capitalism. This was what would be eradicated, replaced with dedication and death if that faith wasn't offered up freely.

There was only so much which could be done to encourage a non-believer.

Jeff's phone rang in his pocket, playing some indistinct tune from the 80s. He whipped it out and thumbed the screen.

"I gotta take this. I'll see you later." He stood and ambled to the door. "Keep me informed."

"You got it." Anand focused on the screen again, and the soft snap of the door faded into background noise.

He exited his email and brought up his Facebook page. He checked the first of his fake profiles for messages, but there were none.

The tweeting of birds outside the window did nothing to soothe him.

He'd spent ages setting up profiles for every security and IT analyst he could impersonate safely. With those accounts, he had access to individuals who were stupid enough to have social media accounts when they were high up in major organizations.

The NSA, CIA, FBI. The world was open, and the little men within the beasts were idiotic enough to think owning an account was safe.

Not if Anand had anything to do with it.

Nothing was sacred anymore. No password or firewall could stand in between him and his target, no matter what it might be.

He logged into his latest creation and a message notification popped up.

It was from Daniel Zang, the 52-year-old NSA contractor with a penchant for Asian girls, apparently.

Anand twiddled his fingers over the keyboard like a master magician, and got into the 'Jia Kailai' mind-set.

Hi Daniel, how are you?

The three dots which signaled Daniel was busy writing back appeared.

There's my favorite law grad. I'm good and you?

Anand considered for a minute. He needed to get to this guy in person. If he could get Daniel out of the house, he could get him out of the way. Anand had been successful so far but Zang's interference into how it'd come about was a risk to Anand's operation.

He wrote back a minute later – let him dangle for a while, increase the tension. *Just tired from work. I've got a question though. Mind giving me some advice?*

Sure, what's the prob? Anand clapped once. He'd called it. Daniel was a lonely middle-aged guy who wanted respect. And fake Jia was more than willing to provide it.

Well, I'm dealing with a network of spam messages and I'm afraid the company's been hacked. I figured you'd know how to deal with this kinda thing. I've got all the knowledge behind me, but I'm a lil worried about how to approach this. I don't want to step on any toes, you know?

Daniel didn't reply for a minute or two, and Anand opened up his profile page and scanned through the pictures of him and his pet dog, Twiggle. How pathetic.

Westerners were soft.

He'd dressed him up in a Santa Claus outfit for the holidays.

What a sad, sad little man. He was the easy prey, the target for Anand's attack. He had the hacker skills along with the social skills most of his underground brethren lacked.

He had to be hard, but living in the U.S. had made it difficult.

A reply popped up.

I totally understand. Look, the best thing you can do is report it to HQ and then proceed with caution. It's difficult when you're in a corporate setting. You can't just shut down emails or use accounts without permission.

Anand laughed out loud. This guy was a bleeding heart. Poor dude.

Thanks. I'll do that. He paused and took a breath. This was the big time – he had to get to Zang before time ran out. *I have another question. It might seem out of left field, though.*

Daniel's reply was immediate this time. *Sure, what's up?*

I'd like to meet up sometime. Get to know you a little better, if that's okay. I mean, this whole online thing is great, but how do I know you are who you say you are?

Anand pressed enter. That last question was a nice touch of irony.

He stared at the screen, willing those three dots to appear.

Booooooonk – whoosh!

His email notification went off and he brought it up instead. It was from the real man in charge.

A cold sweat broke out on Anand's brow.

Time is running out. Bring justice now or you will be punished.

There wasn't a signature, but he never left one. Too risky and totally unnecessary. Anand deleted the email and emptied his trash and spam folders in case, then pushed himself back in his chair.

The pressure was on. He had to get Daniel out of the way and implement the plan, or it would be his head on the chopping board. In the most literal sense of the phrase.

He got up, poured himself a cup of coffee and went back to the desk.

He brought Facebook up again and waited.

Daniel hadn't replied, but at least he was still online.

Five minutes passed. Still no reply. This wasn't ideal. He had to get Daniel out before everything crumbled. He hovered over the computer, debating for a moment, then leaned over it again.

Daniel? Don't leave me hanging. Lol.

That should lighten the mood.

The green circle beside Daniel's name disappeared. He'd gone offline.

Anand stared at the screen for a full minute. What could he do about that? If Daniel had gotten wind of something strange, it'd be over before it began. No, it couldn't be that. How would he possibly know?

Anand slapped the lid of his laptop closed.

Whatever happened, he had to find a way to get to Zang.

CHAPTER 4

click *Today we will see how to* *click* *test the water before* *click* *sharks always sleep* *click* *I don't care what the hell you have to* *click*

Mary sat on the dingy sheets of a cheap motel room flicking through the four available channels trying to find a distraction from her current hell. She had spent a large chunk of the $500 she had left in her savings account – separate from the main current account – to rent this room for a month.

The rental comprised of a bedroom and the smallest possible bathroom that could hold a toilet, sink and shower. A single yellow light bulb barely lit the room, but it made the sheets seem as if they'd been soaked in urine.

There was a strange discoloration on the carpet on the side of the bed closest to the bathroom. Mary had already made a mental note to avoid it. Her laptop rested on the bedside table. She looked at it longingly, but her internet rental fee had expired yesterday and she wanted to save as much as she could for food and emergency.

There had been no word on the investigation into the loss of Mary's pension for a few days. Edward had called upon his supervisors and poor Mary had been bounced around from department to department.

It seemed the company she'd invested with was a sham. When the bank called the authorities to investigate the address, it led them to an abandoned building on the outskirts of the city.

The property was listed as owned by a company called Eco-Tech, which was based in India. After that the trail disappeared. Or so the police officer had told her. In the wake of all of this chaos, her assets were frozen and the bank had claimed the house.

They treated her as though she was a nuisance, not a victim. She flung the remote onto the bed. That familiar headache came on. Mary reached over to the bedside table to grab some aspirin.

Bang, bang, bang.

"Mary Dorowski, this is the FBI. Please open the door. We have some questions for you."

The shock turned into hope: they probably had a lead on her pension! She hopped out of the bed and rushed to the door as quickly as her aged legs would take her.

Two agents stood outside. One was tall and sported the typical long trench coat agents wore in the movies. The other was a heavy-set Latino fellow with a thin moustache and a bald head.

"Hello, Mary Dorowski here. Come on inside. Take a seat anywhere."

The two men gave each other quick quizzical glances before entering the room. The tall one posted himself against the wall next to the television while the fat one took the wooden chair by the table next to the door. Their silence filled the room with tension.

"So, can I get you guys anything? I don't have much, but I have an electric kettle so I can whip up a decent cup of tea."

The fat one spoke first. "No. Thank you, ma'am. I am Agent Luis Perez and this is Agent John Maloney. We're here to ask you some questions and cover some bases with you regarding your involvement with the investment scam."

"Pardon me, sir," Mary interrupted. "What do you mean by involvement? I was not involved. I was the one that got robbed. What are you trying to say?"

Agent Perez cleared his throat and rubbed the back of his hand against his chin. His partner leaned on the wall and didn't meet her gaze.

She was a mother, this behavior wasn't foreign to her. "Now agents, let's not play around here. I've lost my house, savings and patience in all this. I don't have the time nor space to dance around this thing. Whatever it is the two of you are holding back it's time to spill it."

Her outburst made them chuckle. Their chuckles made her head hot and fueled the headache. It must have shown on her face because the fat one quickly turned his laughter into a coughing fit and tried to put his serious face on.

"Well Mrs. Dorowski, in the course of our investigation some information has come to light that has raised some interesting questions. For starters, let's talk about the late Mr. Leonard Dorowski."

Mary frowned, but nodded a moment later. "All right, what about him?"

"He passed away 15 years ago. Is that correct?" Perez instigated and a sharp pain she associated with loneliness cropped up in the center of her chest. Her Lenny, gone forever. She'd see him in heaven one day, at least.

"Yes, that's correct."

"And before that?"

"What do you mean? He was alive before then."

Perez gave a sheepish grin and glanced back at his partner, who folded his arms and bobbed his head in encouragement.

"What did he do professionally?"

"He was in retail. I'm not sure. We didn't discuss his business that often. He took care of the finances and I took care of our home." Mary choked up. She missed her living room, her kitchen, the roasts she'd made there, even after her husband's death.

But the bank had foreclosed and auctioned it off, and here she was in her tiny motel room, sweating after working at a local grocery store. Her life had ended years before she'd die.

"Ma'am, please don't play dumb."

"Excuse me?!" Mary snapped her back straight and glared at the agent. How dare he insinuate that she'd tell him anything but the truth? "What exactly are you getting at here? What is going on?"

She deserved answers. This intrusion was totally uncalled for – as if she didn't have enough stress to get on with.

"Mrs. Dorowski, your husband was a key member of the Gang of 8." Perez stroked the fabric of his worn jeans. "Are you familiar with them?"

Mary shook her head, but in denial of what he'd said, not of the knowledge of the most well-known criminal gang in the U.S.

They were white collar mostly, but they'd use whatever means they had to get what they wanted. She'd seen a special on TV the other day about them, discussing whether they were real or a made-up ploy by the government, a means of distracting the public from its internal issues.

It had all seemed so far-fetched.

"They're a group of criminals who specialize in corporate espionage, money laundering, and insider trading. There were a few murders which have been tracked back to the gang, but there's no solid evidence of that yet."

"I know who they are."

"Oh?" Perez perked up and so did his has been partner. "You do? Wait, of course you do."

"Yes," Mary answered quickly. "I saw a news special on TV."

"I see." It was clear the detective didn't buy it, but she was too shattered to care. How could this be? "Our recent data has correlated the Gang of 8 with some pretty serious illegal activity. Some of which may include terrorism."

Mary went cold. There was no better way to scare her than to say the t-word. Especially with her nephew out there fighting the evil forces in Afghanistan or Syria or one of those rat-infested sandy countries.

What a horrible place.

"Were you aware of any illicit activities while Mr. Dorowski was alive?" The intrusion continued and Mary coughed into her fist.

"Of course not. And there is no chance that my husband would partake in anything of the sort. No chance. My nephew is in the military, for heaven's sake!" Mary was outraged by these allegations. Anyway, what did it have to do with her?

"That's part of the reason we're here, Mrs. Dorowski."

"What do you mean?"

"Taylor Wins is a suspected terrorist. He was part of the Midnight Havoc operation."

"That's silly," Mary snapped, then fanned her face in the heat. "I heard from him the other day, before this all started."

Perez's interest spiked, and he leaned forward. "Are you admitting that you're in touch with a terrorist, Mrs. Dorowski? If you're carrying on your husband's work, then now would be a good time to admit it so we can cut you a break in the legal proceedings."

"Are you insane?" Mary scrambled to her feet."I would never do anything to harm this country. I love this country! I'm a 20th generation American, for God's sake. I can't believe you would say that."

"Ma'am, calm down. These are the questions we have to ask," the partner spoke up, finally. "Your IP address has been a hotbed of activity, and you've been linked with several investment schemes."

"Yes! That's all this is. My pension fund is depleted and I want it sorted it out. I don't know anything about terrorists or criminal gangs. I'm an old woman! I cook and clean and watch *Antiques Roadshow*. You have to help me." She let the last plea resonate in the room, meeting the gazes of both men.

"Let us help you by telling us the truth."

"I am telling the truth. My pension fund was cleared out the other day and I have no idea how it happened. The bank won't tell me anything and I can't – "

"Enough. Mrs. Dorowski, we know that you had money invested with Paradigm Enterprises."

The name rang a bell. It was the investment company she'd used to grow her funds. Or that was the company her lawyer had recommended.

"Yes, exactly. So how can I get my money back?"

Perez glared at her as if she was stupid.

"Paradigm Enterprises is owned by Jeff Aceves. Mr. 8 of the Gang of 8. The man who replaced your husband 15 years ago."

"No." Mary shook her head. "No."

"I'm afraid your story doesn't add up, Mrs. Dorowski."

Mary huffed and puffed for a few minutes.

"Lawyer," she managed to request. "I want my lawyer, William Whitland."

CHAPTER 5

In the last couple of days, Hailey had endured a humiliating onslaught of events. Since the incident had been so public and had happened on school property, not only were Hailey's parents involved but it became a public relations issue for the school district.

Maria and all the boys in the pictures had been arrested on a number of charges, but all of them, except one, made bail by the same afternoon. Being kids of wealthy parents certainly had its perks.

Hailey had to speak to countless officials about what she did and didn't remember from the night of the party. She indicated who she could identify from whom she couldn't. Then she had to repeat all of that for her parents, which mortified her.

She was forced to take the rape kit even though the assault was days before. Being poked and probed for evidence of a crime wasn't something she'd thought she'd experience in her life.

Then there was the barrage of private messages and emails from perverts requesting sexual favors or describing their favorite photo from the incident that was shuttled around as "Hailey Gone Wild".

Some people had hacked her online social channels and uploaded a video of the confrontation at the school on her Facebook page, which was then shared 35 times before she could take it down and block automatic posts to her wall.

The media had even gotten hold of the story and had a field day reporting on the sexual practices of high school kids. Since Hailey was old enough, the initial stories mentioned her by name before Hailey's parents could file a motion with the courts to curb it. By then everyone already knew.

The official media were not the worst of her troubles.

Stories like hers were only interesting for a time anyway and then they tended to blow over. It wasn't like she was a Kardashian. It was the hacking of her social media blog that pushed her over the edge.

The blog was her outlet when things were a little tough in real life. It was her happy place in cyberspace and it had been invaded. There was no part of her left sacred from this attack.

The police said there wasn't much they could do with a backlog of "serious matters to attend to" so Hailey was forced to combat the backlash alone. Whoever had gotten into the account was constantly re-posting video clips from her ordeal in the school's hallway.

Hailey's webpage usually featured inspirational clips she found on YouTube or some of her personal thoughts she filmed or wrote about. This new content caused quite a stir with her loyal followers. The concerned emails and comments filled her inbox alongside the hate mail. It overwhelmed her: the world seemed to crumble away so quickly.

"Why don't you come out you dirty slut!"

There were loud splattering sounds. Missiles hit the house. Hysterical laughter shattered the silence, and a screech of tires followed shortly after. The culprits were gone.

Hailey pulled back her curtains and looked out the window, but the sun had set a while ago. The clouds had covered the sky threatening rain all day, the street lights were on, but it was still pretty dark outside.

A dark-colored pickup truck, with its back tires skidding sideways, rushed around the corner and out of sight. It was probably the football guys from school banding together with their rapist buddies. This was the second time this evening that her dad would have to go outside and clean up what was sure to be a mess of eggs on their front porch.

He'd call the police and they'd have a marked police car sitting outside their house drawing even more unwanted attention.

"Ugh!" She fingered a lilac teddy bear with a deep purple ribbon around its neck which sat on her desk. "That hole would be perfect right about now."

She cradled her head in her hands, tears splashing onto the finish of her small desk. The whole situation made her sick to her stomach. The stress had caused some of her hair to fall out.

She sighed. Some of those kids studied with her. They played games with her. They all grew up together and yet they'd turned against her at the battle cry of one person. It was absolutely crazy.

"Hailey, come down for dinner."

"Be there in a minute, Mama."

She went over to her bathroom, dried her face with a bath towel and headed for the door. An alert went off on her laptop. She glanced back at it – the blog tab lit up on the browser. Someone had either just left a comment under a post or sent a personal message.

In either case, her hunger decided she'd check it whenever she finished eating whatever her mother had made for dinner. It smelled delicious. She made to move off downstairs, but the alert went off again. Then it happened in rapid succession.

Hailey rushed over to her laptop and opened up the blog page. She let her breath out slowly. The harassers were back up to their old tricks and had filled her homepage with video clips again.

She sucked her teeth in disgust and shook her head. It was like this gag didn't get old. The still shot of one of the videos caught her gaze so she took a closer look. Her eyes opened wide in shock. She screamed until her mother and father rushed into the room.

"This has gone too far. What kind of monsters attend that damned school? They cannot get away with this!"

Hailey's father had been ranting and pacing the living room for the past hour. She sat as meekly as possible on the living room couch trying not to move for fear that she would draw his wrath.

She tried to make herself as small as possible and to blend into the beige furniture. The man had walked the same line repeatedly ever since the video was posted. He'd start by the big bay window that faced the front yard and walk over to the mantle place on the far side of the room. He'd touch the mahogany finish and continue his patrol by passing between the couch and the coffee table heading toward the doorway, and out into the hall. Then he would make a jittery, frustrated action and head back by the window. He'd pause for a few minutes, staring out the window before he started the cycle again.

"The lawyer is on his way and I've alerted the police as well," her dad said. Her mother was a fairly heavy-set woman but Hailey hadn't heard a sound when she walked into the room. "Does anybody want anything?"

The question was posed to both of them but Hailey knew that her mother's teary eyes were glued to the back of her head. Hailey shook her head to say no even though her stomach rumbled a bit.

The room had gone silent. Her father stopped grumbling and now she could feel his eyes on her as well. The sickness in her stomach had returned from a short hiatus. There were certain things that parents should never have to see.

Hailey had finally caved and decided to shut down her blog. Whoever hacked her page had decided to post video clips from the orgy. To see herself take part in various sexual acts that she had no recollection of was horrible, but it was made many times worse because it was on the internet for the world to see.

"There are ways we can get back at them, people we can talk to."

"Dad, that would make us no better than them."

"It would make us a damn side better than them, I'd say. Good God, Hailey, they've tried to destroy you. And for what?" He stood still and stared at her, hands on his hips.

"I don't have any answers."

"Why would they do this to you?"

What could she say? She'd had a crush on a boy and her best friend had sought revenge?

"Hailey," he said, and her mother walked in again.

"Leave her, let her breathe, Hon."

He snapped. "I've had enough of this pressure. We can't go on with this kind of attention on Hailey, on the family. It's crazy!"

"Well, what do you want to do? Move?" Her mother hardly ever raised her voice, but she did in increments then.

"Anything is better than this."

This was all her fault. She hung her head and swayed it from side to side, blocking out the view of the worn coffee table, and focusing on her father's bare feet instead.

"This is going to destroy us, you know," he raged on, stomping back and forth. "This has already taken a toll on my – "

"No!" Mama barked and he fell silent again. "Don't talk like that in front of Hailey. Baby," she said, directing that at her, "this is not your fault, okay?"

"Okay," she whispered, but she didn't believe it for a second. This was all her fault.

Someone knocked on the door and gave her reprieve from

her concerned parents. They went to see who was at the door and Hailey took the opportunity to sneak away and go to her room so she could be alone.

She grabbed some mail with her name on it on her way to the stairs. She lit up with the first genuine smile in days. The university had sent her a follow-up letter!

It was a welcomed distraction to think about the good times and fresh slate she had ahead of her. Hailey had already planned in her head how to revamp her social media presences to rid herself of the stigma that'd follow the inevitable court case. She'd create new accounts and bump up her privacy settings. She even played with the idea of going by another name to help throw off people until they had the chance to get to know her before the perception of her past caught up with her.

"The school is far enough from here that maybe no one would find out." She actually laughed a bit at that one. There was a difference between hope and delusion. "People Google people. It's just how things were done these days." Hailey opened the letter and read it as she made her way up the stairs. "Dear applicant, we regret to inform you …"

Water pooled in her eyes and the stairs slid out from under her. The walls swelled so she sat down before she fell backward. Her acceptance to the university had been revoked and she, quite frankly, found the reason to be absolute bullshit.

It was some gibberish about an error in the Admissions Department where more students were issued acceptance letters than there was accommodation for in the classes. But something about it didn't ring true.

She'd been on their online forum for new students this morning and there wasn't a peep about this on the message boards. Her gut said the board had seen the news and heard the rumor that she was a wild girl crying wolf after her dirty deeds had been exposed.

This was it.

She'd unplug herself and withdraw from everything and everyone around her. She curled into a ball on the staircase and, for the first time in almost week, she didn't even bother to hide her tears.

"Ping!"

Hailey was jolted upright by the message alert tone on her phone. The red light flashed. She'd experienced dead silence ever since Maria broke her down in front of the entire school so having someone reach out to her was a surprise. It was a text message.

"Who sends text messages these days?"

She deftly swiped her thumb on the screen and tapped the messages icon. There were other notifications vying for her attention. Goosebumps popped up all over her arms. This was déjà vu. If her eyebrow arched any higher it would become one with her hairline. The text was from an unknown number, but it was probably from Maria or one of her cronies.

Check out all those messages and videos. You could never be Maria. Look at the amount of friends and followers I have compared to you! He would've never wanted a stupid slut like you anyway.

Hailey couldn't believe her eyes. She shook her head. The girl was so dumb and so stuck on herself that she didn't even realize she'd just incriminated herself.

It was like they were so caught up in this thing as though it was a game to play until they were bored. It wasn't like they were seriously affecting someone else in real life. She was a human being.

The message was on the screen staring at her and that energy gave her some strength. They fed off her responses for some form of validation or power over her.

Hailey took a breath and deleted the message. Then she picked herself up off the stairs and went upstairs to take away the other means by which they intruded on her space.

She had veered way too far off course already. Things had already blown up.

But now it was time to bring the war back to them.

CHAPTER 6

Mary was lost. The agents had made it clear that this problem wouldn't go away anytime soon. She was a suspect, their prey, and Len was a criminal.

She couldn't believe it. There was no way the kind husband – her savior and sweetheart – had been a man ruthless enough to steal from others. It had to be a lie.

Mary walked to the front door, checked it was locked (double-locked actually), then went over to the laptop on the tiny desk in the corner of her motel room. Work was hell, the heat matched it, and she didn't have two dollars to rub together.

"It can't be true and I won't believe it." That was the chant she'd come up with to get through the doubts about her husband – and about Taylor for that matter.

The fear of arrest and prosecution hadn't evaded her.

Billy Whitland, her worthless big shot lawyer, was unreachable. The nice secretary she'd dealt with before wasn't at the company and Billy refused to answer any calls from her.

But when they'd met for the first time, Mary had thought he was pretty sleazy. He'd seemed utterly bored by the prospect of her account, checked his short-cropped fingernails for dirt, and literally yawned.

Mary sat down at the desk with a sigh, but it did nothing to relieve her tension. The ticking clock on the wall reminded her of the past, the things she'd lost, the things she'd still lose.

How could this happen to her?

She was a grandmother, for heaven's sake!

"No, I can't focus on this now." She flipped open the lid of the laptop, fired it up and tapped her battered fingers on the desk, waiting for it to load.

She still had cooking, at least. A pastime that no one could take from her. She'd go on Facebook, find a budget recipe and spend the evening creating something fabulous.

That was the ticket! It would take her mind off the drama for sure.

She opened up her browser and clicked her Facebook short-cut. The timeline sprang up with a stream of updates. There was Francine Bejarano's grandchild and Mitzi Berrios had gotten re-married, and at her age – fancy that! Mary grunted her disapproval. Marriage was a one-time thing and she couldn't picture being with anyone other than her Len.

The groom was trussed up like a turkey in his black tuxedo, with a protrusion of red skin peeking over the collar of his white cotton shirt – kind of like wattles – to finish off the effect. He wore a broad smile and clutched her old high school friend to his side.

She was resplendent in a cream-colored wedding dress with a lace ruff at the neck, and plum-colored curls falling around her shoulders. Missy had always been a little eccentric.

Regardless, her Facebook friends seemed to have perfect lives. They were happy, living in suburbia, enjoying their lives without the trouble Mary had. She stretched her neck and wiped a bead of sweat away, then grimaced and wiped her hand on the side of the chair.

This was unpleasant poverty.

There was a broken air-conditioning unit over the door, yellow, mouth gaping at her noiselessly. She'd picked up the remote and slapped it against her palm 20 times before she'd thrown it across the room in a fury. Mary gritted her teeth and glared at the shattered remains. She'd have to clean them soon – leaving them there was unlike her, but she couldn't muster up the energy to get to it.

"Damn it." Mary swore then slapped her hand over her mouth.

She scrolled down, her envy and anger growing by the second. Ah! There was an ad for budget recipes on the sidebar. She moved the mouse over, but the timeline updated and she stopped dead.

Horrid pictures of a teenage girl having sexual relations with several men popped up on her feed.

What on earth?

"Who is this girl? What a horrible little slut." Mary clicked on the link.

Teenager partakes in orgy at party, parents and peers horrified as videos go viral.

The headline said it all, but she read the article anyway. This girl, a teenager in Brazil, had been a star student and an apparent good girl until her secret life had been recorded and revealed by several of her peers.

There were no names, but Mary couldn't believe what the world had come to.

She'd been accused of a crime while vicious loose teenage girls went around sullying their own names. The girl didn't appreciate her freedom and the effect she'd had on her family! She didn't care at all, judging by the screen captures from the video.

Mary couldn't bring herself to watch it, though it was there at her fingertips.

Should she? No, of course not. That was vile.

She made to click on the ad again, but another line in the article caught her eye – it was an instant update.

Orgy Teen denies all allegations and will go to court over slander.

Red-hot rage bubbled in Mary's belly. The girl was clearly copulating with the men in the images, but she had the cheek to deny it? To pretend that she hadn't done it, when it was clear she had?

It was too much for Mary to take.

She opened up her Outlook and entered the email address for CNN.

To Sarah Mcdaniel,

I was browsing Facebook when I happened upon several images and an article about a young teen in Recife, Brazil. Honestly, I was horrified by the content of the article. It appears that this young woman (lady would be a stretch) had participated in several orgies with men and has had the cheek to deny it. She is determined to take those who brought the video out to court, even though she has been clearly implicated in the actions. There's video evidence of her escapades splattered across my Facebook feed as we speak.

I sincerely believe that this kind of activity is unacceptable and that it should be brought into the public eye so that behavior like this can be discouraged. Teenagers these days are out of control, and hiding this information from parents will only encourage the depravity to continue. I ask that you will do a special on this girl and her horrific acts to discourage this wanton behavior in other children. These are, after all, the future leaders of America and I am frankly terrified for what will become of our beloved country should we let the level of discipline in our local schools and homes slide.

I have attached a link below, so that you may view the horrific video for yourself.

Sincerely,

Mary Dorowski

She took a breath, read the content through a few times, then added the link at the bottom of the email and clicked send. That would teach the horrid teen. Now she wouldn't be able to hide from her deeds so easily.

How anyone could lie that blatantly was beyond her. The truth was obvious.

Mary stretched and gave a terrific yawn. At least the negativity of someone else's life had distracted her from her own, even if it was for a few minutes. She finally clicked through to the ad and scrolled through the recipes on the page.

There was a honey-glazed pork recipe here. It might work quite nicely. Or perhaps a Thai-inspired stir fry.

There was a lot you could do with minimal ingredients.

"Mrs. Dorowski?" A man called through the door. There was a knock and the door knob rattled.

What now?

"Yes, who is it?" She stood and shut the laptop.

"Mrs. Dorowski, open the door. It's Agent Perez. We need to talk to you immediately."

Terror erupted in her stomach. She glanced at the window, the door, the bathroom, but there was no escape that would carry her away quick enough. The agents knew where she lived. They'd never leave her alone.

What choice did she have but to speak to them?

She walked to the door and opened it. Perez and his surly friend stood on the threshold, they both seemed serious, and the fear jumped up several notches.

The agent took his hands out of his pockets and clasped them behind his back.

"Ma'am, I'm afraid you're going to have to come with us."

CHAPTER 7

For the last three days, Debra had stationed herself in front of the family television trying to get more information on what'd happened in Syria. No one from the military has contacted her with any information about her husband, but every news channel ran the breaking news report every five minutes.

No one knew much, and the channels were surprisingly mute about actual details. They'd been unable to get reporters close enough to get anything but hazy footage of the remains. Rubble, smoke, there were lumps on the ground, but the details were too unfocused to make out what they were. Debra had known the instant she'd seen it.

Those were bodies. Bodies that hadn't been removed or looked after. What if Taylor was one of those bodies? Lying lost in the Syrian desert, the wind sweeping dust over his skin, grains clinging to his lifeless eyelashes.

She gripped her stomach and doubled over.

The neighbors had been a great and intrusive support to her in this time. A few of the ladies from the army wives' support group had taken it upon themselves to take care of her and Shannon.

Susan, Charlotte and Regina kept dropping by to offer their

sympathies and with the annoying persistence of a swarm of mosquitoes. Eventually they infiltrated her fortress of solitude and took over her home in true military fashion. They had cleaned, cooked, did some laundry and even took turns babysitting for the past few nights while Debra mourned Taylor.

The rug had been pulled out from underneath her. He was gone and he wouldn't come back, and she didn't begin to know how to talk to Shannon about it. Debra was lost. She couldn't do this on her own. She wasn't strong enough.

Debra shook her head and breathed deeply, head bobbing. Her eyes drifted closed.

Bang! The hive lost no time breaking the calming silence with bustling chatter and the slamming of pots and pans.

"Good morning to you guys too." She whispered it. "Thanks for checking whether I was still alive."

She reached out to pick up the remote from the coffee table, but her fingertips barely brushed the smooth plastic and knocked it to the floor.

"Ugh. Perfect." She rolled over on her side and picked it up from the hardwood without having to get up. Taylor could be stuck somewhere under some rubble, unable to move and unable to call for help. It was a morbid thought.

"How can there be no news at all? Where are you T?!"

She held the remote in both hands and took the television off mute.

Channel 1 had broken the news that an unexpected terrorist

attack on a United Nations humanitarian effort in Syria had left thousands of people dead or missing. As a result of what seemed to be seven simultaneous explosions, the parliamentary building, three embassies, the Sahara Hotel and the camp sites for the international military forces present in Syria were obliterated.

News reports indicated that jihadist troops backed by the Islamic State were responsible for what was referred to as 'the most coordinated and devastating attack to occur in recent history'. The eyes of the world had been drawn to what the media called "Midnight Havoc."

Relief efforts had been deployed within hours. Some military personnel had been sent from the army base in Coppell. The men had been instructed to take part in the effort to stabilize the situation, but the primary initiative was to bring any Americans involved back to home soil.

Their wives made promises they would find her husband and bring him home. Debra prayed with all her being that Taylor was alive, but deep in her soul doubt had crept in.

The news bulletin never actually confirmed Taylor as one of the dead but he'd been spotted with the humanitarian group that entered the U.S. embassy a few hours before the explosion. They hadn't been heard from since then.

Some survivors had been pulled from the rubble as well as a number of bodies. Different news stations had been broadcasting images and videos from ground zero, which showed relief officials and civilians working together to clear the rubble. Over the last couple days there had been sporadic breaking updates whenever identifications were made and, for this reason, Debra refused to move from her spot on the couch.

Heavy curtains were drawn to block the sun from shining through the living room windows. The light would scorch her weary eyes. She'd cried hard and hadn't slept properly in days. Her hair was a frizzy mess from frequent assault during anxious, tense moments.

The blue pin-striped apron and white sundress she wore from Sunday morning were creased. She'd worked the remnants of a blue dish towel into twists and knots.

The whispers of the wives preparing lunch in her kitchen drifted to her ears.

"How could she just sit there like that? When Jeff was missing five years ago I certainly didn't wallow in it and forget about my kids."

"The woman hasn't even updated her status on our group page. Like her husband is the only husband to have ever been missing. She's probably just fishing for attention right now." Another voice added.

The first voice responded. "Pfft! Guess who needs attention – Shannon!"

There were murmurs of agreement at this last charge.

"Forget them." Debra said to herself. "They don't understand. Stupid gossipy hens. They don't understand. I can't do this without Taylor. They don't understand. I don't need this right now …"

Debra got up from the couch and flew into the kitchen. Her sudden appearance startled the three women. Before they could utter a word Debra gave one even-toned command.

"Get out of my house witches."

Four days later...

"Did you enjoy your dinner sweetheart?"

"Uh huh. It was de-lich-us. Mrs. Claire cooked it?"

The way she pronounced the word 'delicious' always made Debra smile. "Yes she did Honey."

"I like pasta with chicken meats," Shannon said then leaned forward and placed her palms on her mother's cheeks, "and Mommy you look so pretty and clean."

Such blunt, innocent honesty made Debra laugh. It had been the first time she'd bathed and washed her hair in days. She could imagine what the transformation looked like. She'd taken the anxiety of the last few days particularly rough. Taking that bubble bath with her daughter was the uplifting experience she'd needed to get out of her funk. Shannon rubbed her eyes and yawned.

"Are you quite ready for bed?"

Shannon murmured, "Yes Mommy."

"Good. Sleep tight."

Debra gave her daughter a gentle kiss on her forehead, then tucked her little frame into bed under her favorite pink-trimmed sheets that her father had given her last Christmas. She couldn't have fathomed at the time that it would have been their last holiday as a family.

No one thought that it'd be their last time posting a family Christmas album on Facebook for their friends and family, which over the last three years had become a tradition.

Debra reached over to click off the pink lamp on her daughter's nightstand to hide the tears welling in her eyes, but Shannon was fast asleep and snoring lightly.

Shannon's soft hair fell across her forehead and she brushed it back and planted a kiss on her forehead. Daddy wasn't coming home and Debra couldn't change that. She couldn't make everything all right.

Tears spilled down her cheeks.

Debra was thankful because she didn't want to explain these tears to her daughter. She'd already put her through enough and she'd been so resilient through it all. Even in this, the darkest moment of her life when her world was off balance, here was this sleeping ray of sunshine trying to light up her world.

She sat on the edge of the bed watching her daughter sleep and choked on the welling tears. This wasn't supposed to be her life.

Their doorbell rang. She peeled herself from her daughter's side, tiptoed across the carpeted floor and closed the door as lightly as she could behind her. Debra fixed her bathrobe and moved quickly toward the door. She glanced at the clock in the living room as she passed the entryway. At 10:20 p.m. whomever it was better have a good excuse for coming by so late and unannounced to boot.

"If it's one of those darned army wives I'm going to rip her primped and curled head right off."

She peered through the peephole of the front door and a chill gripped her heart. It flowed out to her fingers and toes. Her breath was caught somewhere in her chest. The pain of dry tears pricked her eyes.

Time halted and the distance between the two sides of the door stretched into infinite space. Her right knee banged against the door and she grabbed the frame to keep herself off the floor.

Things were foggy. She could barely hear the knocking on the other side of the door over the crescendo of white noise in her ears. She had to open the door and get help or pass out on the floor alone, and risk Shannon finding her like that.

She took the house keys off the hook on the wall next to the front door. There was no feeling left in her fingers. Her arms felt like they weighed 40 pounds. She fumbled with the keys. Finally, she had the lock undone and used the last of her strength to swing the door open.

There were three men in black suits on her doorstep.

"Mrs. Wins, we have a warrant to search your home."

She'd thought they were here to tell her Taylor was dead.

"What is this about?"

"We regret to inform you that your newly deceased husband,

Taylor Wins, has been implicated in the Midnight Havoc incident. He is a suspected traitor and terrorist." The foremost agent stepped over the threshold and she stumbled back. "I'm going to have to ask you to stand back."

"No."

"Mrs. Wins, step back this instant or we will be forced to remove you."

The walls closed in, the blackness came with it. She collapsed to the floor on all fours, breathing hard.

Then she blacked out.

CHAPTER 8

It was about 7:30 on a Saturday morning. Just two days since Jia had lost her position at the firm and that 'afternoon off' had turned into a bona fide pity party.

She'd called up the five girls that she used to roll with at the university and, under the guise of a mini-reunion, arranged a bar hop on Friday which culminated in a club experience that would go down in infamy if the alcohol permitted it.

They took pictures at every bar to post online. Guys flocked to them at every stop because they were dressed to the nines in form-fitting dresses that stopped an inch or two below their bottoms.

Although none of them were loose, they all enjoyed the free drinks and attention that came from showing just enough skin. They'd finally called it quits when the club closed at about four that morning. The five of them were so drunk they practically fell over each other when they clambered into one taxi with the plan to have the cab drop each of them off at their respective homes.

Being in such cramped quarters with the only people in her life that she had any measure of closeness with was the tipping point. Jia broke down and spilled everything she'd been holding in, to her friends.

To her surprise when she had finished exposing her vulnerable side, and thought that she'd receive some support and encouragement, what she got was a deafening silence. The atmosphere in the cab became very uncomfortable.

They didn't say a word, Jess stared out the opposite window and feigned a small cough. Liz gave an awkward laugh and Pamela leaned her head back on the seat and closed her eyes. They'd reeked of booze and cigarette smoke, but she'd needed that support from them.

Thankfully, Jia was the first stop. She got out of the cab in a fury and slammed the door as hard as she could. All that ran through her mind was the consistent emails and messages that had passed between them over the years they'd been students and study partners.

The countless frat parties, long nights in the library, slumber parties after bad breakups and efforts to keep in touch after graduation seemed to mean nothing to these superficial American girls who obviously had no idea how to be true friends.

There was no way Jia saw her night ending with her curled up on her couch crying into her glass of red wine watching the sun rise above the cityline.

It was officially 24 hours she'd been awake and, although her body craved the sweet release of rest, her mind raced, even on a night's worth of alcohol. The sun was completely visible in the sky and warmed the glass of her apartment's window.

She sat in the window seat with her forehead against the pane, watching her street come alive with activity.

Mrs. Branson, her neighbor in the apartment next door, strolled down the road with her hair done up in a quiff to envy a news reporter. It bobbed with each step. Jia couldn't find the humor in it, though she loved people-watching.

Tears formed again. Would she have to move back into her aunt's apartment in Brooklyn? She'd built a healthy savings account that'd support her for a couple months, but only barely. Her breath fogged up the glass. It ruined her view of the street.

How irritating. But then, what wasn't? From the fact that underpar excuse for a computer scientist Greg had her job to the woman from the apartment across the street who got up at the crack of dawn every morning and insisted on walking her dog on this side of the road, and leaving it's terrier poop up and down the street.

She lobbed a half-eaten apple at the walking duo.

"Shoot!" She exclaimed. That old woman was the landlord's sister. She scampered away from the windowsill hoping she hadn't been seen. "Ugh. Now I'm going to lose my darn place over a piece of fruit and some dog poop."

Jia flopped down onto her sofa. She reached between the cushions for the remote control and the phone rang. She glanced at the clock. Eight in the morning, which meant it certainly wasn't her parents calling and she didn't have anyone else to check up on her today.

She dragged herself off the couch and into the kitchen. Bits of ash dropped all over the floor as she hastened to find the phone. At some point she'd decided the best place for the phone was in the garbage.

It was covered in pasta sauce and bits of spaghetti. Jia held the phone with two fingers and grabbed a paper towel off the roll to clean it off. The phone continued ringing. The phone was still pretty greasy after some vigorous cleaning, so she just laid it on the table and answered it on speaker.

"Hello, this is Jia Kailai speaking."

"Jia! How are yuh? This is your supervisor … err … I mean ex-supervisor Justin Greene. It has come to the company's attention that you may have taken some hard drives and flash drives when you left yesterday. Those drives potentially contain information that is sensitive to the company and its clients. So, we need a couple of those back so we can inspect them or Paradigm Enterprises is prepared to press charges to have them taken from you."

A few ocean breaths later she felt a little calmer and was a whole lot more grateful for those meditation classes she'd taken last year. It'd taken every bit of self-control Jia had left to maintain professional etiquette and not tell this obnoxious prick where he could shove the hard drives.

Not only were these people calling to demand items she had bought with her own money, but this man had the audacity to threaten her.

"Well, Mr. Greene, it is too bad that you seem to have forgotten that I did minor in Law at University. I know my rights and I know that you have no right to demand my property without due cause. You and I both know that nothing I handled during my time at Paradigm was classified information. I did not have access to anything directly associated with the law branch, investment services group nor international management group. It was straight up coding, programming and glitches. So what could you possibly want my hard drives for Mr. Greene?"

There was dead silence on the other line. Clearly this pinhead didn't expect her to put up a fight. It occurred to her that she'd never gotten a proper explanation as to what she'd done that would jeopardize the company's clients. "By the way Mr. Greene, since I have you on the line I would love to know what I did that warranted my dismissal."

His response was stuttering gibberish. This riled up the fight in Jia even more now that she knew she had him on the back foot. She took a deep breath as if she was ingesting inspiration and went back on the attack.

"Mr. Greene, I am starting to think that something is amiss. I refuse to submit my hard drives for inspection without a proper explanation as to what is going on."

There was that familiar abrupt click before the line went dead.

What could possibly be so important that they'd go to such lengths to get her drives? Just about everything she'd dealt with while she was with the company had already been moved onto the company's servers and she hadn't been doing anything pressing when she'd been dismissed.

Jia immediately went back into the living room and grabbed the drives from her work bag. She hooked them up to her laptop one by one. The first two had nothing interesting on them, but on the third she discovered an encrypted hidden file that refused to open using any of the typical cracking methods.

The challenge made Jia smile. She put on her glasses, pulled her long black hair into a neat ponytail and got to work.

About five hours and just as many cups of coffee later, Jia was sitting in front of her laptop staring at hundreds of files from all three of Paradigm's sister companies. She could tell that the files had all been put onto the drive a few days ago and updated remotely ever since. But there wasn't much digging she could do beyond that, not from her home PC at least.

She had no idea how these files got onto her computer or what they were collected for, but it was clear that if this was the reason for her dismissal then she'd been set up and the culprit could get away with it.

The now clean phone began to ring on the desktop beside her. She answered half expecting to hear someone from Paradigm calling again. The deep voice sounded vaguely familiar.

"Good afternoon. Am I speaking to Ms. Jia Kailai?"

"Yes. This is she."

"Ms. Kailai this is Agent Greg Davoli. I'm working with the FBI and I need to speak with you immediately."

It was the first time she'd had a full conversation with Greg in the four months they'd been around each other at Paradigm. He seemed like such a bland wishy washy kind of guy, but now she realized he was a whole lot more than that.

His voice was deep and strong. His tone was authoritative. It was a complete opposite to his persona in the office, and it sent a thrill up and down her spine.

He was too different and she felt a little loopy for not realizing that he wasn't what he'd seemed.

They didn't talk long on the phone. He'd given her instructions to be ready to leave her apartment in a few minutes and she was too embarrassed to mention that she hadn't yet showered or eaten yet, even though it was after one in the afternoon.

Fifteen minutes later, Jia was nowhere near ready. She was in the kitchen wearing only a bra and a towel and swearing at the toaster, which held her bagel hostage. Her hair wasn't brushed, most of her casual clothes were in dire need of laundering and she had dragon breath so strong that she could melt wax.

A black SUV pulled up in front of her apartment, and the agent gave two crisp toots of the car horn.

Jia shoved her head through the window so he could see her. "Be down in just a minute!"

She bashed the toaster until it gave out, snatched up the smoking breakfast treat and tossed it between her palms. Puffs of steam billowed from the top of the shower, and she ripped the curtain back, scraping it along the rails.

Jia unhooked her bra, leapt in, rammed the bagel in her mouth and washed like a housekeeper on a coffee kick.

Another 15 minutes later someone banged on her door. Jia froze in her tracks. She wasn't sure if she should open the door or crawl out the fire escape window. The banging continued.

"Suppose someone sent a shooter?" she thought. "I saw this movie. The shooter kills helpless woman by blasting through the door with a shotgun." She stood in the middle of the hallway glaring at the door.

The peep hole darkened. Whoever was outside could now see her. She leapt out of the way and rushed over to the window. She was halfway out onto the staircase before the agents introduced themselves and asked if she was okay.

They hustled her out the house and into the back seat of the Cadillac Escalade. She was stuck between Greg, who was pretty gorgeous up close, now that she got a good look at him, and another agent who was so huge that he could probably pinch her skull between his thumb and index finger.

They were on their way to their hotel room where they had set up a small base of operations for processing the data for the case they'd built against Jeff Aceves. He was the founder of Paradigm, and one of the major stakeholders of the parent company Europa Inc.

She'd seen him pretty regularly around the office. In her short time of observation, Jeff was usually very hands on when it came to interactions with the employees and was always the front face managing the company's contracts and portfolios.

He was the kind of guy who would wear designer clothes and

make them look average. The typical persona one would find in the business arena but, according to Greg, this man had a dark side. He was a member of an elitist organization called the Gang of 8 which had kept the city in a chokehold since the late 80s.

However, Jia couldn't figure out what all of that had to do with her. They could've just taken whatever was on her drives and left her out of it.

"Ms. Kailai, your association with Mr. Aceves and his activities has not gone unnoticed. It is best that you work with us and make a deal for yourself now before it's too late."

CHAPTER 9

It'd been just over two weeks since she'd received official notice that her husband had been killed in the blast at the base. Debra's life had been thrust into a constant downward spiral. Her foundation – her husband – was gone, but she'd been informed she'd have to vacate the family home by the end of the month while Taylor's history was investigated for treason.

She reeled from the blow because she had no idea what to think. The military believed that files that had been retrieved from his personal computer were evidence he had secretly been providing information about military plans and position to a third party.

The discovery had serious implications in the wake of the terrorist attack in Syria and while the case was investigated, Debra wouldn't be eligible for any of the usual military benefits.

She lost the house and their assets were frozen, but thankfully they gave her a small stipend to survive on while they pried into their lives.

There were always men in the house, exploring, investigating, and military-issue cars parked in the street. Sun glinting off their windshields, obscuring the men inside.

Although Debra had tried her best to keep the news under

wraps by not spending time on her social media networks, and limiting the time she spent with the other wives, the word still spread quickly. Within a matter of days she and her daughter were treated like pariahs in the community.

Mrs. Perks had even campaigned with her two minions to orchestrate a coup d'etat and usurped her position as President of the Army Wives' Support Group. Now she couldn't go to the supermarket without enduring the stares and whispers of those who were once friendly neighbors.

It was too hard to keep a brave face for Shannon who was blissfully oblivious to what had happened. Debra hadn't told her that her father was officially dead. She sat beside her in the car singing some pop song at the top of her lungs.

It was beyond irritating. She was in a living nightmare and she couldn't pinch herself hard enough to wake up. They passed their neighbor outside, working on the flowers in her front yard. Mrs. Myers was the retired wife of a veteran soldier who'd babysit Shannon whenever Debra and Taylor decided to have a date night. Shannon loved her.

"Hi Mrs. Myers! Do you have cookies?" Shannon called out to her in her usual excited fashion.

But their extremely patriotic neighbor chose to scowl and ignore an innocent little girl, just because her father may be a national traitor. Shannon frowned, then her face crumpled and tears welled up in the corners of her eyes. Debra punched the off button on the radio, and looked down at her dejected daughter.

She parked the car, grabbed a bag of groceries and went back over to the neighbor's house. When the older woman saw her coming she tried her best to get out of the garden and back into the house, but her age showed, and Debra was right up in her face before she could make it to her feet properly.

"Where the hell do you get off being such a witch to a little girl? She didn't ask for any of this. She was just doing what she was supposed to do. She's a good girl. Takes care of her family. You know what? Screw you! Screw ALL of you back-stabbing people."

Debra walked away. She made sure to trample the perfectly manicured grass and stamp in the flower bed. She got to the sidewalk, then an idea struck her, and she looked back at her neighbor, who was still rooted to the same spot she'd left her in. Shocking that pretentious old bat had been satisfying. She'd be gone in an hour or two so she decided to give the woman one last piece of her mind.

She splattered those pale-yellow walls and streak the paned glass windows with a dozen eggs.

Then she let Shannon out of the car and left the groceries in the car. They were supplies for the motel, where they'd stay during the investigation. She went inside and up to the room to finish the last of her packing – Shannon's cases were already in the car.

A Skype call came through on her phone.

"Shannon, bring Mommy her handbag."

She layered her clothes on top of each other, folding haphazardly. The phone rang on.

"Shannon, I said to bring my bag, darn it!" Debra shrieked. She patted down a shirt and spun on the spot. "What the hell is wrong with you, Shannon? Can't you hear me calling you? Are you stupid or something because –"

The short rage only got her a few steps because Shannon appeared in the doorway struggling to hold the handbag in her little arms. Her eyes were wide and teary.

"Sorry Mommy. I couldn't reach it."

The phone continued to ring. Debra walked toward her daughter and bent down until they were almost on eye level. She took the bag from the little angel and rested it on her legs, then used her thumbs to gently wiped away the tears that escaped her eyes.

"Thank you. Mommy is sorry, ok?" Shannon nodded meekly. "Go ahead. I'll call you when it's time to go."

The phone had stopped, but now it rang again. Debra stood up and placed the bag on her dressing table while she rummaged about in it to find the persistent little device. She looked at the caller ID. She didn't know the number but she answered the call anyway.

"Hello?" There was no response. The only thing she could hear was the sound of heavy traffic in the background. "Hello. Who the hell is this and why do you keep calling me?"

"Hmm. You're feisty for the wife of a traitor."

Her blood ran cold. There was a new shock in store for her at every turn.

"Who are you and what do you know about my husband?"

The person on the other end of the line chuckled then disconnected the call.

"What fresh hell is this?" Debra whispered. "This cannot be happening to me."

Her mind raced and she steadied herself on the dressing table. Taylor was gone, and she was stuck with Shannon, raising her alone. He was the one who'd wanted the life in the suburbs, to serve his country, and she'd gone along with it. Not because she wanted what he did, but because she'd wanted him.

She still did.

And things had changed now. She loved Shannon with all her heart, but part of her felt things would've been easier without the four-year-old.

"Mommy? Are you okay?"

"Yes." Debra gritted her teeth in frustration. How was she supposed to handle this without Taylor? "Yes, I'm fine. But your Daddy isn't. He's gone away now and I don't think he's coming back."

Shannon's soft steps came closer, blocking out the anger and replacing it with pain. Absolute pain. Debra's knees went weak and she collapsed to the floor, bringing the picture frame with her.

It was a photo of the day Shannon had come into the world. Debra held the little bundle and Taylor had his arms around the both of them, smiling up at the camera. So happy and so alive.

"I can't do this anymore." She didn't know where to go or what to do.

"It's okay, Mommy." Shannon knelt beside her and stroked the top of her head. "Daddy will come back. I promise."

This angel. This little girl who knew so little but saw so much. How could she be angry with her? How could she be mad about having her when she was the only person keeping Debra sane?

She dried her tears and placed a palm on Shannon's cheek. "Let's go."

Ten minutes later they were in the car, but the anger hadn't abated. She wanted Taylor back, but she refused to believe it was possible. She was alone and she didn't want to be.

They pulled out of the army base and drove hard, heading away. Somewhere, she didn't know where yet. Any motel would do until she could figure this out.

Shannon sat beside her in silence, staring out the window. Her big eyes glassed over with sadness and guilt punctuated Debra's emotions. She shouldn't have told her, but what choice did she have?

"I love you, Mommy."

"You too, Dear." But she couldn't bring herself to feel anything.

She glanced in the mirror and cold fear settled in her heart. There was a black SUV following them. Debra swerved into the right lane and turned a corner. Sure enough, the SUV followed.

"Mommy, I'm nauseous." Shannon piped up again.

"Be quiet."

She turned another corner, and another. The SUV trailed behind them, caught in traffic. This was her chance!

"Mommy."

"Shannon, shut up!"

The pressure built inside her. She had to get away. She had to get Shannon to safety.

She swerved again and sped up, driving as fast as she could in a narrow road between two buildings. She checked the mirror and sweet relief spread through her. She'd lost them.

"Sorry, Shannon. Mommy had to fix a problem."

But Shannon didn't reply. She had one hand on her stomach and the other over her mouth. Debra pressed a button and the passenger window slid open. The little girl stuck her head out and vomited noisily onto the street.

"Oh Baby, I'm sorry."

Debra looked up and her grip tightened on the wheel, fingers numbing slightly.

The SUV was back.

CHAPTER 10

"You're crazy." Jia shook her head and placed her hands on the smooth steel table with a sigh. It made sense, though. Pieces of the puzzle clicked into place in her mind, even though she wanted to deny them.

That puzzle didn't create a Swiss vista or conjure up images of ships in the dock, rocking gently side-by-side. Rather, it was a total loss, a faded photo of New York City in shambles, concrete and brick crumbling from the buildings.

That was her damn life.

"Unfortunately, no. I've spent the last months undercover for this," said Greg, scratching at a mole on his neck. He was a lot more intelligent than she'd given him credit for, and kind of cute too, in a slightly nerdy way.

Obviously, the dumb intern thing had been an act to throw people off his scent. He'd done a good job of it – she certainly wasn't stupid and it'd fooled her.

"The Gang of 9?"

"Eight," he answered, slurping from a Styrofoam cup. The coffee steamed, fogging up the lenses of his square glasses. He slipped them off and pocketed them.

"And Mr. Aceves is part of this criminal gang?" This was what her hard work had boiled down to: an interrogation in some indistinct room with a full-length mirror on the wall. God, she looked terrible. No amount of bagels and two minute showers would remedy the dark circles under her eyes. Where had the years gone? The opportunities?

"We have information which suggests he's Mr. 8. The lowest on the hierarchical totem pole, but still a criminal. He's aimed himself at investing schemes, but he's headed in a new direction of late."

"A new direction? Look, that's great for you and everything, but what's it got to do with me?" Jia didn't touch her coffee, though she'd love it. She didn't want to lose concentration for a second. This was too weird.

"I'm getting to that," Greg answered, glancing at the mirror on the back wall. It was obviously a one-way mirror. Who was back there, watching?

He pushed himself from the chair and paced over to a water cooler in the corner, then poured himself a cup of that too.

Greg came back to the desk without drinking it. "You've got information on your flash drive. It's got an encryption on it."

"How did you –?" But she already had the answer to that question. He'd put it there. It made sense. He was the only one who would've had access to any of her things. They worked in the same department, used similar equipment. It would be simple for him to get his hands on a flash drive and mess around.

Greg shifted himself into the chair with a small grimace. "I planted the information there. The encryption is from Paradigm and we needed that information."

"You got me fired," Jia said, pointing at him with a long, red fingernail.

"Actually, no. I only planted that evidence after you were removed from the company. You were fired because of your involvement with," Greg paused and rifled through documents in a cardboard folder on the desk, "a one, Daniel Zang. He's an NSA operative."

"Dude, I've got no clue what you're talking about." She grabbed the Styrofoam cup and squished it a little too hard. Coffee slopped onto the table and over her hand. "Oh, darn!"

Greg fished a handkerchief from his pocket and gave it to her. She mopped up the liquid and cursed under her breath. This was the worst Thursday she'd had since, well, since ever.

"Honestly, I've never met anyone named Daniel Zang before."

"You've been in contact with him on your Facebook account. There's no use lying, Ms. Kailai, we have the transcripts." Greg pushed a page toward her and she snatched it from his grasp and lifted it to read the words there.

Her eyebrows climbed her forehead, arching into Disney character proportions.

"What the hell?" There was her name and this Daniel guy's, laid out with several messages, some of them were familiar, a blink past friendly.

"You mean to tell me you have no recollection of this?"

"I don't have any social media accounts except for like Instagram, or something. I happen to think they're the friggin' bane of the world's existence."

Greg gave an appreciative grunt. "Paradigm thought you had contact with Zang, who was working to undo Aceves. You can connect the dots from there."

"But I've never met the guy before. I've never even heard of him." Jia tugged at her hair in frustration.

Greg drank from the water and scraped his chair forward, leaning in close. "So, let me lay it out for you in braille. You were working, communicating even, with several men and women high up in Aceve's operation. Whether you knew about the investment schemes or not is beside the point. We can't eliminate any suspects right now."

"What are you saying?" Jia's heart went cold. "That I'm some kind of corporate espionage suspect?"

"I'm saying that if you're involved with the Gang of 8, you're in some serious trouble. And if you aren't, you're in even deeper trouble."

Jia rapped her knuckles on the cool steel. She'd had enough of this. Her life had fallen apart around her ears and she couldn't let this get worse. What the hell had she done to deserve this?

She'd worked hard, hadn't she? She'd done her best, treated people right, kept her damn nose to the grindstone to avoid straying from the path. She'd avoided relationships as well.

She'd missed out on so much, just to get ahead, only to find out it'd been a pipe dream all along.

A couple tears welled up and she placed a finger under her eye to stem them. "What kind of trouble?"

Greg watched her, measuring her, and his expression softened. "The 'dead' kind of trouble."

Jia gripped the edge of the table and glared at him, mouth snapping open and shut like a fish out of water.

"We've got several analysts examining the contents of your flash drives to help us piece together a case against Mr. Aceves."

"A case for what? What is he doing?" She just wanted out of this situation. Out and away. But if she got that, she had no clue what she'd do next.

"He appears to be targeting a specific company. Insider trading."

Jia snorted. "That's literally something I have no interest or knowledge about. You realize that right?"

"Jia, I'm afraid that doesn't make a difference."

"Oh please, you're not 'afraid' for me. You don't give a crap. I'm tired. I'm going home." She rose, but he raised a hand and several men in suits entered the room and lined up against the wall.

"That's not going to happen."

"You have nothing to hold me here." Jia had rights and she damn well knew them.

"You're not free to go, but you won't be staying here. We've got you a room in a hotel, for your own protection."

"I refuse," she said, stomping her foot.

"You realize that Mr. Aceves is a hardened criminal? If he finds you, he will kill you. It's best if you stay with us."

"What?"

"You'll be under guard all day and night, for your own protection."

Jia folded her arms. Things were fast spiralling out of her control, and there was nothing she could do to regain power over the situation. "You think these suits are inconspicuous?"

"I'll be the one escorting you," Greg said, standing as well.

Jia stomped her foot again, then stilled it. It was no use acting like a toddler and throwing a tantrum. She didn't have a choice but to go with Mr. Davoli and do what the men said.

What other options were there? Run? Get killed by her ex-employer?

It was unbelievable how quickly everything had gone sour. Her life was in the toilet.

Greg pointed her to the door and she turned on her heel and marched out, disappointment guttering through her. This was what she'd become: a washed-up suspected criminal.

Jia ground her teeth and refused to meet Greg's eye. They'd seized her possessions, interrogated her, and now she had to do what they said, what they wanted.

Or so they thought.

Jia set her jaw. She wasn't a pushover and she refused to be a failure.

There had to be a way out of this, and she intended to find it.

They got out into the parking lot, and Greg directed her to his car. She feigned interest in what he had to say about Aceves, but kept her eyes open. Night had fallen in the interim, and the lot was clear of any other agents.

Greg took the keys out of his pocket.

Jia dived at him and grabbed at the keys, knocking him back a few feet. She dashed for the car.

"Hey! Don't be stupid, Jia. You'll never get out of here."

But she didn't care. She had to try. She wrenched the car door open and fumbled the keys into the lock. Greg was close, walking toward her as if he had all the time in the world.

Jia jammed the keys into the ignition and tried to start the car, but nothing happened. The engine sputtered and died.

He was closer. A couple seconds and he'd get to her.

Jia turned the key again and pumped the gas. The engine thrummed to life.

CHAPTER 11

Billy Whitland was at the end of his tether. After Lorraine's dismissal, everything had gone downhill. The spam had continued, in spite of his best efforts to find and eliminate the source.

And Mr. Neveu had reported him and requested different representation because he'd continued receiving correspondence and documents from Billy's email address.

Which was, of course, impossible since Billy hadn't sent him anything and had resisted opening his inbox because of the threat of spam.

He scrubbed the back of his neck, wiping away the sweat of the day and glancing up at his busted a/c. It wasn't technically broken, but the white block didn't put out enough cool air, and it whined when he clicked the buttons on his remote.

Stupid thing. As if he didn't have enough to deal with without sweating himself to death. He roasted in his own juices, a pig ready for the eating.

He had a court appearance tomorrow. The firm doubted his abilities after Mr. Neveu's allegations of misconduct, and had launched an investigation into just what had happened.

Billy would get the results tomorrow, as well.

He snatched the phone off its cradle and dialed the extension for the IT department.

"This is Jonah, how can I help?" It was the same dweeb who'd called him a while ago to let him in on the spam in the first place. Billy tried swallowing the instant brew of anger in his gut, but it was a futile attempt.

This creep needed a fat smack across the head.

"Hello, this is William Whitland. I'd like to report an issue with my email account."

"Mr. Whitland," Jonah said, the click of typing filled Billy's ears. "It seems your account has been shut down."

"What?!" Had the company closed his email account?

"Yes, I'm afraid we received a large amount of complaints regarding spam from your account. We were forced to close it without your permission, because you didn't respond to the cease and desist order."

He needed that account. He received statements there, corresponded with clients – other than Mr. Neveu, of course – and it held the history of the emails between him and the CFO of CialCorp.

"Do you have any idea what you've done?"

"I'm sorry, Mr. Whitland, but we were forced to follow corporate protocol," Jonah said, tone hardening.

"Screw corporate protocol! I demand you retrieve the information from that account at once."

"That's not possible. All the information associated with that account was erased because it posed a security risk to the company."

A security risk? That didn't sound like straight up spam. There was something fishy going on here.

"Fine," Billy snapped, "then open another email account for me."

"I'm not at liberty to perform that task, Mr. Whitland." Jonah stopped typing and his voice grew louder, as if he'd shifted the receiver closer to his mouth for privacy.

"Why the hell not?" Billy had fast lost his patience, but he didn't care. It was impossible that he'd fallen this far, this fast. He'd been lined up for the Leather Lounge, for Pete's sake.

"I can't authorize the creation of a new email account until after your court appearance, Mr. Whitland."

Billy shoved himself backward in his office chair and glared at the computer screen. His desktop background was the company logo.

"Will there be anything else, Mr. Whitland?"

Billy didn't grace him with an answer. Instead, he slammed down the receiver with such force that the desk shook. Years of dedication and schmoozing with clients, and this was what he got.

He'd been faithful. He'd paid his dues. And now his loyalty had been called into question.

He stood and walked to the damn air conditioning unit. No one had been along to fix it, even though he'd reported it broken a few days ago. He wasn't a priority for the firm, anymore.

There had to be a way to fix this. He had contacts in the government. There had to be someone he could call to work it out and back him up.

Billy clicked his fingers and snatched his jacket off the back of the chair.

Daniel would know what to do. He was an old buddy from college, who'd ended up working with the NSA. If anyone could get to the bottom of this espionage deal, it would be him.

He strolled to the door, past the empty receptionist's desk – they still hadn't gotten him another receptionist – and out to the elevator, before he took out his smartphone and dialed the number.

The elevator dinged, and he stepped inside and rode it down to the basement level while the phone rang.

"This is Daniel Zang, who's speaking?"

"Hi Daniel, it's Billy, how are you doing buddy?" Automatic suck-up mode kicked in right away.

"I don't know anyone named Billy. I think you have the wrong number."

"No, come on. William Whitland? We went to college together? You dated Wanda and I stole the mascot's head after a frat party. Any of this ringing a bell?"

Silence yawned on the other end of the line.

"Oh yeah, Billy, right. How are you?" But Daniel still sounded cold and different, somehow. The hairs on the back of Billy's neck stood on end. What if he couldn't get the NSA man to help him?

The steel doors of the elevator slid open and he stepped out into the underground parking area. His BMW – cherry red, of course – was further down, so he set off walking.

"I'm not so good, Daniel. I've got a bit of a problem on my hands here."

"Oh," the other man replied.

"I'm a lawyer working closely on an account for a technology company. They're announcing their IPO later this year. You might be familiar with them: CialCorp?"

"Yes, I am familiar with them. What's happened?" Concern colored the NSA agent's reply.

"My email account was used to spam most of my clients and colleagues, and to send sensitive documents to the CFO of the company. I've not touched the account in ages, and I found out they closed it today for security reasons."

"Seems suspicious," said Daniel.

"You're telling me. Would you consider meeting up with me to discuss this. I've got a hunch that whoever hacked my email is probably after something bigger than just sabotaging my career." Though they'd done a mighty fine job of that. The sooner Billy proved his innocence in this, the sooner he'd be in that Leather Lounger sipping martinis and counting his millions.

"Billy, I'll see what – "

"Hold on a second," he interrupted, and pulled the receiver from his ear. His footsteps echoed in the lot, but he could've sworn he'd heard something. And it wasn't a car starting.

"Sorry, you were saying?"

"I'll see what I can do. I'm not sure how I'd be able to help you."

"I thought it was something you could look into. I mean," Billy said, gesturing grandly, "who knows how deep this thing goes? Why would someone hack my account?"

There it was again. Billy glanced over his shoulder, and the blood in his veins slowed to a glacial ebb. A hooded figure darted behind a pillar, a few cars behind him.

This was too creepy.

"All right, I'll set up a meeting time," Daniel said.

"I'll have to call you back," Billy whispered and hung up before the agent could get another word in.

He hurried along, tucking the phone into his pocket and casting glances back every couple paces. The blur of black following him drove his blood pressure through the roof.

He wheezed, belly jiggling slightly from the exertion. He didn't want to break into a run and encourage the pursuer to do the same. Where was the damn BMW?

Billy searched the lot, steps faltering for a moment, and the scramble of pursuit followed suit. Sweat stung his eyes, but he didn't wipe it away, widening them instead.

What did the guy want? To scare him? Mission accomplished.

He fumbled his car keys out of his pocket and raised the immobilizer, punching the button until the keyguard creaked with protest.

But the blip of the BMW didn't come.

Billy raced off in the other direction and footfalls rushed up behind him. There was nowhere to go, nowhere to run. He had to find the car. He had to get out of there!

There was hot breath on his neck and fingers clawed at his back. He tossed his jacket to the side and sprinted on, struggling out of the man's grip.

The car? Where was the car?

He punched the button again.

Blip, blip.

There, to the right. Billy changed direction and the chaser followed him. The vision of his BMW appeared. Billy pick up the pace toward his car.

He was almost there, he was almost safe. He pumped his arms furiously, and the frantic scratching at the back of his cotton shirt disappeared.

"Ha!" He panted in fear and triumph and reached out for the door.

A man in a suit appeared in front of the car door.

"Good afternoon, Mr. Whitland."

CHAPTER 12

Jia was done with this. She'd had enough of the mystery, enough of the danger. Enough of the damn handcuffs.

Okay, so there weren't any actual handcuffs, but still, the motel room was enough of a trap.

She rolled over in the single bed and glared at the lumps which were Greg Davoli, lying across from her entangled in his own stained sheets. The FBI could've at least sprung for something classy.

Jia could've done better on her shoestring budget, and she was fresh out of a job for crying out loud. This was what her life had become. So much promise, yet here she was in a tiny motel room, across from an indifferent agent who had a bad case of the snores.

This was not her life.

She shook her head hard, throwing a silent mini-tantrum on her pillow to get the excess anger out.

She wouldn't let this happen to her. She didn't buy that rubbish about Aceves coming after her. It was obviously just a fabrication to get her to stick around because she was a suspect.

For what though? Greg had mentioned an IPO and insider trading, but it was a vague explanation at best. He'd suckered her into staying. Jia gathered the blankets in her fist and pulled them aside.

Jia Kailai was nobody's sucker.

She rose slowly, glancing surreptitiously at Greg, tracing his shape beneath the blankets. His snores roared away at an unbelievable decibel level. The man needed a sleep clinic.

She had to get out and away, make for another state and get her life back together. Aceves could be Gang of 8, or he could be the sleaze ball she'd met in the hallway a few times. Either way, she was outta there!

Jia swung her legs over the edge of the bed and hopped to her feet, graceful as a cat. Those years of dance lessons had paid off. Granted, she'd hated every minute of the uppity ballet teacher's instruction, but at least she was light on her feet.

She shuffled to the low, pine table positioned against the wall, slathered in putrid egg-yellow paint, and swept up her handbag. There wasn't much left in it, but the FBI had given her back the hard drives and flash after they'd cleaned it out.

They had more courtesy that the idiots at Paradigm, at least.

She grunted sourly and swung the bag up, slipping the strap over her shoulder. Greg was too busy inducing an earthquake to notice. Jia whipped out her purse and rifled through it, but she was criminally short on cash, and there was no way she'd stop at an ATM until she crossed a state border. She needed gas money, and quick.

Greg's wallet was on his bedside table, and a spine of guilt wedged between her eyes. Stealing wasn't her thing, but desperate times and all that.

She crept over and snapped it open, then pulled out a handful of twenties. It would have to do until she got where she needed to go.

He gave an almighty snort and she dropped the wallet, snatched up the keys and hurried to the door, slipping the money into her bag.

She stole away, out into the night, and took her first breath in what seemed like days. She was free as a bird. The strong scent of gasoline mingled with old urine, and her lips curled down at the corners. That was nasty.

Freedom didn't smell so good.

"Now what?" She scraped a couple strands of her hair behind her ear. She didn't have a real plan, other than to get out of there. There wasn't a job waiting, or even a few family members. God knew she couldn't rely on her friends anymore.

She strolled through the lot outside the motel, the soft breeze tickling her skin, bringing the fragrance of fall leaves with it – that was a grand improvement over the parking lot odor, but there was also the mulch undertone to complement it.

Greg's Hyundai was a couple spaces over, but she wasn't in a rush, though she should've been. There was nowhere to go. The minute she got into the car, it would be the beginning of a new chapter. She'd be on the run from the law.

Did she have a future left to salvage?

Jia bit her lip until it hurt, then gave a curt nod. She had to make this work. There wasn't a chance she'd give up this easy. She jangled the keys and hurried towards the car.

A dark figure stepped out from one of the motel rooms nearest her.

"Good evening, Ms. Kailai." It was a man's voice, mocking in its thickness – the consistency of phlegm.

"What do you want?" She couldn't keep the fear from her question. She edged toward the car, extending the keys. If she could get in the car … but that hadn't worked last time. Greg had gotten to her before she could escape.

And she had the hunch this guy wouldn't give her a light reprimand.

"Give me the flash drive and no one gets hurt," he said, ambling toward her. His gait was easy but assured. It scared her even more.

"Stay away from me," she said, and tried unlocking the car door.

"Don't do anything stupid," a second voice warned behind her, and she jumped about a foot in the air. She backed into the side of the car and glared at the two men.

"I don't have anything." She put her hands in the air. This was unbelievable. Greg couldn't be right. He couldn't!

"Wrong answer," the nearest thug said, then dove at her. He knocked the keys from her hand and punched her square on the jaw. She fell to her knees, totally disorientated, then keeled over sideways.

Her forehead grazed against the gravel, cutting her skin. Her jaw was a throbbing mass of agony. A face appeared beside hers and rough hands wrenched her bag from her shoulder.

He turned it inside out and the contents spewed across the ground, her lipstick and tampons rolled in opposite directions.

"Here it is," he grunted, retrieving the flash drive. She didn't have the mind to protest.

"I'd put that down if I were you." Two loafers, shined to perfection, approached across the lot.

"Kill him," the thug holding the flash drive ordered. A scuffle broke out, the scraping and thwacks resounded in the open air. There was a thump and Jia gave up hope that Greg could save her.

"You're next," said Greg, and the man with the flash drive disappeared from view. More shuffling and knock out sounds came next. Jia's breath whistled through her nose.

Another heavy thump Greg connected with the thug's jaw, blood splattered on the ground as the thug slumped beside her, eyes half-glazed. Greg stepped on his Adam's apple.

"Who are you working for?"

The man spit on the shoe with a snarl.

"Do you like breathing? Because I have no problem crushing your windpipe." Greg's foot inched forward and the guy gave a strangled noise.

"Aceves," he croaked. "He wants the information back."

The information on the drive. It had to do with that company

Greg had mentioned. Jia couldn't piece the puzzle together in her mind. Why would insider trading matter this much to Paradigm? The company was rich, it made no sense.

"Aceves can dream on."

"What are you, a fed? You look familiar," the thug said. Perhaps he'd seen Greg at the office.

Thwack! Greg's foot came down hard on the guy's jaw. He passed out immediately.

Greg leaned down beside her and lifted her into a sitting position, he stroked her cheek gently and checked her eyes. "Jia? Are you okay?"

She couldn't muster up a groan of concession.

"Right, we need to get out of here."

Jia frowned and he grasped her meaning.

"I called in a couple agents to clean this up and collect, but we need to move motels. If they found you this easily, there must be someone on the inside giving them information."

It was as clear as mud to her, but what could she say? She raised a hand and touched her jaw, then snatched it away again. It was on fire, but it wasn't broken or hanging skew.

Greg Davoli gathered her up in his arms, unlocked the car door and slid her into the passenger seat. He crossed to the driver's side and sat down, then started the car.

"Oh," he said, pulling out of the lot, the headlights illuminating the two bodies sprawled on the tarmac, "and don't ever try to run from me again."

The warning made it clear he didn't trust her. Jia gripped the armrest and worked her jaw without a sound. Anxiety fluttered through her stomach.

Where was he really taking her?

⸗ ⸗

Street lights flashed by in a blur and the speedometer climbed past 60 miles per hour. They were on a residential road but it didn't seem to faze Greg. His mouth was drawn into a thin line, hands gripping the wheel and the strap of his seat belt tucked under his armpit instead of over his shoulder.

"Where are we going?" Jia asked in a semi-slur. The throbbing in her jaw had subsided after she'd popped two aspirins she'd found in the cubby of the Hyundai.

"Another motel."

"I deserve to know where you're taking me! I have rights, you know." Jia unclipped her safety belt and he shot her a sideways glance of distilled irritation.

"You have nothing but a gangster on your back and a lot of explaining to do." Greg took a sharp turn, checked the rearview, adjusted it and focused on the road again. He wore a cool exterior, there were no lines of anger on his cheeks, but the set of his shoulders was … antagonistic.

That anger rolled off him in waves.

"I told you everything I know." She was tired of this. He obviously thought she was some kind of spy or something. "Is this because I'm Chinese?"

"What?!" Greg swerved slightly, then regained control. His upper lip twitched – was that mirth? "Oh come on, Jia. Get real. This is because you had sensitive information which Aceves wants. You're obviously involved in his operation, otherwise you wouldn't have tried to run and you wouldn't have his cronies on your tail."

"That's a butt load of assumption in one stupid sentence."

"There were several sentences," he pointed out, cracking his neck, "and it's pretty obvious there's something fishy going on." He pumped the gas and the car zoomed down the road, chewing up tar beneath the wheels.

"Something fishy." She repeated it, the slow burn of rage building alongside the pain. "Something fishy. All right, buddy, you want to know what's fishy?" She reached over and pulled the handbrake up.

The car skidded and Greg wrestled it onto the verge of the road. It came to a grinding halt. Smoke rose behind them, then swept over the car, filling it with the acrid tang of burnt rubber. Greg's knuckles were white on the wheel. A minute later he switched off the engine.

"Are you crazy?" He snapped it out.

"No. I'm angry. How stupid do you think I am?"

"I don't know –"

"That's right," she interjected, "you don't know. You don't

know shit and neither do your buddies in the bureau. I'll let you in on a little secret, Davoli: I haven't done anything wrong!"

"That's yet to be proven."

But she was already on a rampage. "You were the one who pulled me out of my apartment without any real evidence that I was involved with Aceves or anything else. You were the one who brought me out here on this wild goose chase. And you're the one who won't do me the grand courtesy of telling me what the hell is going on!"

"I told you, insider trading, CialCorp's IPO."

"Whatever. That doesn't even make sense. Why would a guy like Aceve's care about something like that?"

"To buy shares in the company when they're cheap? To get ahead of the curve?"

"I'm aware of the definition of insider trading, Greg, just not why Aceves would go to the trouble of hunting me down for whatever information he had. That was a copy you made, it wasn't like you took his only files on CialCorp."

"Because he doesn't want to get arrested for white-collar crime."

"White-collar crime. Oh well, that explains it all then. The thugs trying to kill me, the NSA getting involved. Has to be just about the IPO. You're not telling me something."

"I've told you what you need to know," Greg answered, eyes focused on the road, though they were still parked.

"I want to know why I'm really involved in this. I want to see that Facebook account. If someone's using my name, I have the right to know." She wouldn't stand for this anymore. She deserved the answers, and she'd be damned if she'd let him whisk her off to different motels each night without getting her answers.

"I don't think so."

"I've lost everything I worked for. An entire life of build up to a future that no longer exists because of this. I deserve answers!" She slammed a fist onto the dash and he actually flinched – the first sign of weakness she'd seen thus far.

"Okay, okay." He sighed and reached behind his seat. He brought out a laptop case, and unzipped it. Five minutes later he'd hacked into Jia's fake profile and had Daniel Zang's conversation up. He gave her the laptop so she could drive.

She scrolled through it, tapping on the touchpad to read random texts.

"What the hell?"

"And you've never seen any of this before," Greg stated, folding his arms.

"Of course not." She pointed at a picture on the screen. "What's this? Hey, that's a picture from Debra Wins. I haven't spoken to her in ages!"

They'd been friends in college, but Debra had always been set on a life with Taylor.

"Wait a minute," she said, clicking on the picture and bringing it up, "this is a picture of Taylor. He must be in Syria or …" she trailed off. "Oh my God. That thing on the news. That thing, what was it?"

"Midnight Havoc," Greg whispered it, almost in reverence.

"He wasn't in it, was he? He wasn't killed?"

"I'm not sure, Jia." But there was something in his voice which gave her pause.

What had they said on CNN? 'Midnight Havoc had devastated American troops giving relief in Syria.' Devastated was the word. That could only mean one thing.

"Poor Debra. She lived for that man." Jia shook her head. "This makes no sense. So, whoever created this fake profile knew I was friends with her. And they were talking to some guy from the NSA." Chills spread up and down her spine, and the hairs on the back of her neck stood on end.

"I know what you're thinking but –"

"It's a terrorist."

"Jia, let's not jump to conclusions here."

"Come on, put two and two together. They're talking to the NSA and they could've used this picture to identify the position of Taylor's outfit. What the hell is that about, and what does it have to do with Aceves?"

"Okay, assuming you didn't strike up a conversation with Daniel Zang and this is a fake account, it doesn't mean Aceves is a terrorist."

"I didn't say that. It just doesn't add up. I didn't have access to any of the information you hacked and placed on my drives. I didn't do anything wrong."

"You must've had some information."

Jia's eyes widened. "It was you. You were fiddling around with their files and they probably thought it was me, because, let's face it, you seemed useless in the office."

"Thanks."

"Yeah, no problem," she said, waving him off. "And once they saw the connection to Daniel Zang … but they wouldn't know about that connection unless they had a hacker, or the person who was impersonating me is in the company. Which means they might be terrorists."

"I'm sorry, but it's too much of a leap. I need stronger evidence than that." Greg started the car. "We'd better get you out of here."

"I need to speak to Debra."

Greg pulled into the road and gave her a quizzical look. "Why?"

"Because if Taylor's dead, I need to know. And I've got to know when she added me on Facebook. Can you get her number for me?"

Greg indicated and turned into a side road, traveling along at a more moderate speed. Jia watched him, wary of what he'd do or say next. He didn't glance at her, but tension was etched into his demeanour. He hunched over the wheel.

"I'll see what I can do."

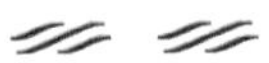

"What the hell is this?" Jia held up the flash drive and waggled it at Greg.

"A flash drive," he answered in a monotone. He returned to his TV dinner – beef stroganoff – and concentrated on the tiny screen. CNN was on. The motel he'd chosen didn't have any other channels.

"You kept the files." She'd found it in his jeans while he was in the shower. Yeah, it was kind of sleazy to go through them, but he'd left her no choice. He was clammed up tighter than, well, a clam.

Greg chewed on bits of steak and ignored her. He scooped up rice and creamy sauce and deposited it in his mouth.

"Answer me, Davoli," she growled. He had a strong jawline and she had to stop herself from admiring it. She hadn't had a boyfriend in years, she wasn't sure she was capable of real emotion anyway. The last guy had dumped her because she'd been 'a work-obsessed harpie with the emotional range of a goldfish.'

"I have the files from Paradigm, yes. But it's all encrypted, anyway."

"Why do you have it?" Jia folded and unfolded her arms. Then paced in front of him, tracking across the beige carpet.

Greg paused, with the fork poised above the plastic tray. "Because I'm an FBI agent working on the case."

"Why didn't you tell me?"

"Because I'm an FBI agent working on the case."

"Argh!" Jia threw her clenched fists up in the air and brought them down with a slap. She tugged at her faded jeans, the flash still clutched in her fist.

"Mind you don't break it," he warned, directing a creamy-ended fork at her.

"You're not even mad I took it. What's wrong with you, robot man? Don't you care I have the drive and I could mess up your career. Or your little plan to keep me here?" Jia paced back and forth. She wanted a reaction out of this guy, she was tired of his mystery.

Greg stood and took the remnants of his dinner to the trash can, then dumped it in. "I don't know if I care anymore."

"What?!"

"Nothing. Give me the flash drive back." He strolled up to her and held out a hand. She resisted the urge to take it, but pocketed the flash drive instead.

"I think I'll hang onto it for now." Maybe she could use it as some kind of bargaining chip, with either the FBI or Aceves and his Gang of 8.

"Suit yourself," Greg said, and went to sit on the bed. This wasn't as exciting as the movies she'd seen. The kind with fugitives on the run and non-stop action, not CNN-watching agents and flash drives.

"I need to use your phone."

"What for?" Greg stretched and yawned, kicking off his shoes.

"To call Debra."

Davoli froze and gave her a blank expression for an answer. He reached into his pocket and brought out an ancient-looking cell. It wasn't even touch screen. He handed it over.

"I need her number, too."

"It's on there. I called in a favor while you were in the shower." He gave a wry grin and she blushed.

Jia flicked her hair back over her shoulder and dialed the number. She held the phone to her ear, forcing down the plethora of butterflies, locusts too, in the pit of her stomach.

"Who is this?" Debra answered, though she sounded worn and harsher than when they'd last spoken. Maybe that was just the stretch of years between the two events.

"Hi Deb, it's Jia. How are you?"

"Jia." The woman repeated, drawing the syllable out. "Jia. Jia Kailai?"

"That's correct," she answered with a winning grin, as if her old friend could see her.

"This is a pleasant surprise." Debra didn't seem all that pleased despite the sentiment. "What can I help you with, Jia."

"I – I'll level with you. I'm in a bit of trouble and I need a couple answers. Can you help me out?"

"I don't know, kiddo," Deb answered, and Jia gave a fist pump – that was the name she'd called her at college, a pet name. "What kinda trouble are we talking here?"

Debra was hard as a rock. Her tone, unyielding.

"The federal kind," she answered straight and glared at Greg, daring him to interrupt or snatch the phone away. He rolled his eyes at her instead.

"Yeah, I can relate to that."

"So listen, when did you add me on Facebook?" Jia jumped right into the good stuff.

"Uh, wow, that's a random question. I have no idea, maybe a couple years ago."

"A couple years?!" Jia gasped and Greg bolted upright, shaking his head and motioning for her to quiet down. Heavy steps fell outside the external door of the room, which led into the parking area.

More thugs?

"Yeah, I think so. Why?"

"Because you need to unfriend me," she said and Greg made swift chopping motions with his left hand. "There's – uh – a problem with my account and I don't want you to get involved."

"I'll do that. Jia, I'm a little confused here. You called to ask me about your Facebook account and what else?"

"I guess I just wanted to catch up on the news, you know. How's Taylor and the little one, what's her name?"

"Shannon. And Taylor's dead, thanks for asking," Debra replied, tough as nails. She wasn't the same person after all, but she'd provided the answer Jia had feared.

"God, Debra, I'm so sorry to hear that. How did he –? When did he –?"

"Heard of that Midnight Havoc thing on TV? Yeah, he was killed in that and to add insult to injury, the feds are pinning it on him."

"Pinning it on him? What do you mean?" Jia swallowed several times and Greg slid off the edge of the bed.

"The government thinks he committed treason and betrayed the position of the troops."

Jia grabbed the back of a rickety motel chair and lowered herself into it. If only Debra knew what had really happened.

"I take it from your silence you're as shocked as I was. Anyway, I've gone off the grid and I've taken Shannon with me. I won't subject my child to this kind of abuse and I'm tired of marching to the beat of this cursed country's drum."

"Slow down, Deb. What are you getting at here?"

"You realize they're everywhere, don't you?" Debra whispered it and Jia gripped the table to steady herself.

"Who is?"

"The feds, criminals, terrorists. The world is a cesspool, a melting pot of human fondue scum and I refuse to let my daughter grow up in a world like this. I'm going to put a stop to it."

"How?" Jia met Greg's gaze and flinched away.

"I've joined a group, you might've heard of them. Anonymous."

Jia drew in a sharp breath and pushed up from the table again. "I know them. At least, I've heard of them."

She walked to the window and peered out into the parking lot. There was a figure perched against a door opposite theirs. The L-shaped setup of the building didn't provide much privacy.

Anonymous was a hacker cell, working outside the function

of the law. They were synonymous with revenge crime, anti-government action, and most recently, a declaration against terrorism.

"You get to wear one of those cool masks?" Jia joked though inside she was a tempest of anxiety. The white mimic of the anonymous mask was an anarchist symbol and it was unbelievable that Debra – vanilla, husband-adoring Debra – had rallied to it.

"I'm serious, Jia. This is a cause that needs support and I'm determined to provide my skillset. Shannon will have a better future once we take on the establishment and create a better world order."

The woman was delusional.

"I don't know."

"I do. We're combatting ISIS, the Gang of 8, the NSA, CIA, FBI, child pornography, consumerism. All of them are going down and Anonymous will be responsible for it."

Jia froze and lowered her voice to a whisper. "Did you say the Gang of 8?"

"You should join us."

"I thought they were situated in Europe." Greg stood behind her, inches from her shoulder, straining to listen in on their conversation. She didn't move off because the heat from his body gave her the tingles.

"There are Anons everywhere, Jia. We've set up a little base of operations in Washington and it would be great to have another experienced computer science engineer on board. You know your way around the web and the law."

"Yeah, you could say that." Jia traced the outline of the flash drive in her pocket.

"Anyway, give it some thought. Call me back if you're interested and we'll set something up. What's your email address?"

Jia recited it to her over the phone. What if the call had been tapped? An itch sprang up in the back of her mind. She wasn't supposed to care about these things, she wasn't supposed to be in this position.

"Thanks for your offer, Deb, I'll give it some serious thought."

Click.

The other woman was gone, whether to hack sites or take down social media accounts, who knew? Jia had lost her power and position; her education and hard work meant nothing.

"What did she say?" Greg spoke up, breath tickling the back of her neck.

Could she do it? This might be her shot at a new life – one where she was useful again, where the hours meant something to her.

"She invited me to join Anonymous," Jia answered truthfully. She bit her lip and turned to face him, examining his wide mouth and the slight hook to his nose.

"Jia –"

"I'm going to do it."

"You're crazy if you think joining an anarchist hacker group will solve your problems," said Greg, wrinkle lines appearing on his forehead.

"Then I guess I'm crazy. I'm doing it."

"Jia, it's not safe and it's illegal, to make matters worse." He reached out and grabbed her arm, creasing her long-sleeved checked shirt. "Think about what you're suggesting here. If you do this it will change your life forever, and not in a good way."

She wrenched her arm from his grip and shoved the phone at him. "Change my life." She threw back her head and gave a belly-aching laugh. "You think I planned any of this? I graduated summa cum laude from university, I was the star intern at Paradigm and I lost everything. Wanna know why?"

"Stop, calm down and let's talk about this."

"Wanna know why?" She repeated, shaking off his feeble attempt at grabbing her for the second time in as many minutes. "Because you and your pals at the Bureau just happened to infiltrate my company. I did nothing to deserve this, but work hard and try making a better life for myself and my family."

"Yeah, well we can't all live fairy tale lives. All right?" Greg snapped, and tossed the brick of a phone onto the desk. It fell with a clunk but didn't break apart.

"Fairy tale lives? My life wasn't a fairy tale! It was one hundred percent hard graft from the minute I arrived in this God-forsaken country."

"Watch your mouth." He warned, wagging a finger under the tip of her nose.

"What are you going to do Fed-boy? Arrest me? Oh wait, wait a second," she said, placing a hand on her cheek and dropping her jaw in mock consternation, "you already did that. For nothing!"

Greg's chest heaved and his nostrils flared, but he didn't back down. That icy façade had dissipated.

"I am doing my job." The sentence was strained, pushed between his teeth to leak between them.

"Yeah, and I don't have one because of you. You've got your future planned out, probably a white picket fence and wife to wash your dirty socks, and I've got nothing. I've got nothing because of you." She could picture it and the pang of jealousy didn't help.

"You can't blame me for this."

"Then who should I blame? Who the hell should I blame, Greg?" Jia sighed and dropped her shoulders, bowing under the pressure of the past few days and the ruination of her plans. "I can't stay trapped in this with you."

"You're a suspect. You don't have a choice." He was too close for comfort, his lips were plump, wet where he'd licked them.

"Oh, I do and I've made it. I'm going to Washington to meet up with Anonymous."

Greg scrubbed at his hair and growled, "What do you think that's going to achieve? They can't help you get your job back, or your life for that matter."

She patted the pocket of her faded jeans. "I've got the encrypted files on CialCorp. With this, I can make enough money to do what I want and bring Aceves down."

"I won't allow it."

Jia strode to the bed and picked up her handbag. "I didn't ask for your permission." She walked to the door, but he pushed in front of her, blocking her exit.

"I can't let you leave," he said, sombre resolve expanding from him and into her mind. He was on the job, this one. He'd do what it took to delay her and not because he actually wanted her around, but because he had a job to do. Federal agent through and through – she'd been a fool to dream he'd react differently.

"Get out of my way," she commanded. He didn't move.

"Wherever you go, whatever you do, I'll find you and bring you back. Don't you get it? This isn't about your plans or your life. This is bigger than us."

"So the few should suffer for the good of the many? What pseudo-psychological nonsense is that?" Jia strafed sideways and dived for the door, but he blocked her again. She circled slowly and he did too, until her back was to the door.

"Aceves needs to go down and the FBI will be responsible for that. Vigilantism won't solve anything."

"Open your ears and listen for a second: it's not just Aceves. There's more to this than you're willing to admit, because you're afraid of the implications." She reached back and gripped the doorknob. He came in fast and close, then gripped her wrist. His lips were inches from hers. "I don't have the luxury of fear," Jia said. "All I've got left are my guts and my brains and what I can do with them."

"You've got so much more than that. Once this is over, you'll be able to start a life for yourself." Greg brought himself closer, pressing her against the door with her hand pinned behind her back.

"This will never be over. If it's not Aceves it's someone else. The entire world is burning. Have you turned on the news lately? Have you seen what's out there? Ebola, ISIS chopping off journalists' heads, Russia half-annexing bits of Ukraine, war, terror, strife, poverty. Boko Haram executed an entire village in Nigeria for God's sake! And do you think anyone cares?" Jia shook her head, brushing her nose against his by accident. "Aceves and CialCorp are drops in the bucket, and that bucket is filled with lawlessness and despair. With destruction."

"Stop and think for a second. Think about what your life will become."

"Oh, I am thinking. For the first time in my life I'm thinking clearly. I studied for a future that no longer exists because of people like Aceves. I intend to take back the power."

"Jia, it won't work. There are too many wrongs to be righted. You'll destroy yourself this way." He cupped her chin with one hand, still holding the other behind her back, and made her meet his gaze.

"As much as I'd like to believe you've got my best interests at heart, I know it's a lie."

Where had that come from? What did it matter if he had her best interests at heart? She took in shallow mouthfuls of air and avoided those lips.

“I do care. I do have your best interests at heart,” he whispered, eyes fierce with passion he’d hidden from her.

“Greg, you can’t stop me,” she murmured, finally letting herself focus on his mouth, its corners turned up in a half-smile.

“Watch me.”

He brought his lips toward hers and they met. His kiss was soft at first, but they got caught up in each other, melting into the taste, the heat. She inhaled his scent; it was clean and woody, everything a man should be. He brushed her cheekbone …

“We should get some rest.”

Jia couldn’t fall asleep. Heck, she couldn’t even close her eyes. This was disastrous. She’d fallen for this guy by accident – it was Stockholm syndrome at its finest, except he was a good guy, the kind she’d wished she’d had a chance to date.

She was trapped by her feelings for him, though she’d tried to ignore the attraction and mutual respect. Jia chewed the inside of her cheek and tapped her fingers on the bedspread.

She sat up slowly and got off the bed, then tiptoed over to get her stuff. She checked that the flash drive was still in place.

Jia wrote a note and placed it on the pillow beside his head.

I’m sorry.

Then she was gone.

CHAPTER 13

He'd spent two hours yesterday arguing with the incompetent IT staff. Somehow, somewhere along the line Billy had stepped into the proverbial dog poop and had been smearing it through his life for three months.

The head of the department was a relatively young guy named Justin Greene. He'd been hired by the firm fresh out of graduate school when they started taking on high-profile clients. His specialty was security. He made sure all their digital files were protected behind firewalls and encryptions so complex NSA would have issues hacking into their information.

However, the employee's email accounts were not under such strict protection. Justin had said he would try to trace where the hack had come from, but he couldn't make any promises since the account itself had been placed on hold.

That lousy Jonah had told him it was closed, when really it was frozen in cyberspace and Billy didn't have the access code. Justin's litany was a polite way of saying that he was screwed.

Last night had been sleepless. He'd scoured his memory and the paper documents he'd printed for CialCorp, checking for sensitive information that may have been alluded to during correspondence.

Billy groaned and forced the door to the coffee shop.

At one point he'd started writing his letter of resignation and ended up throwing his PC on the floor. Thank God his wife – a notorious hippy with a wealth of underarm hair – had convinced him to buy that thick, hideous rug. At least it was useful for something: cushioning the laptop from destruction.

He ambled up to the counter, and eyed the bimbo chatting to the guy in the line ahead of him. His head pounded – he'd emptied his bottle of Mount Gay Rum 1703, which was a Christmas gift from his first wife and their son.

Blondie motioned him over with an overly enthusiastic wave. God help him.

"Hi Billy! The usual right?"

He wanted breakfast, not the breakfast club. It was unusually light this morning, which made Billy smile because he wouldn't have to wait as long for the grub. However, that meant the chirpy little blonde working the register would have nothing much to do but blabber on about how *The Book Of Concepts* had 'like totally changed my life, ya know?'

He hid his disgust behind a forced grin."Hello April, I'll have my usual breakfast croissant and coffee, but throw in a chicken club sandwich to go, as well."

"Whoa there. Someone's a big spender today, huh?" She cocked one hip, with a twinkle in her eyes, and punched the buttons on the register.

"Yeah." There were no other words. He stood staring at her. She'd said it with the biggest, dumbest smile Billy had ever seen. If it wasn't for his buddy who owned the joint and was head over heels for this woman, he would've pressed him to fire her a long time ago.

April squinted at the prices on the board behind her, then turned back to him. "All right Billy-O, that'll be $13.01 for a chicken club, breakfast bagel and a cup of Joe. I'll have it sent over to your regular table." She printed the receipt and slid it across the counter.

The last person who'd called him Billy-O had been 10 years old and he'd bitten him on the cheek, little barbarian that he'd been. Nobody messed with a Whitland in the sandbox. Except the world was a much bigger sandbox, and he couldn't go around biting everyone who offended him.

"Things going well at work, Billy-O?" April leaned over the linoleum while he brought out the money.

"Fine, thanks." He said it in clipped sentences, then handed her $15. "Keep the change."

"Thanks man!"

He hurried off to his table. The chick probably thought he'd tipped because he liked her, meanwhile he wanted to get away from her as fast as possible.

He'd phoned Daniel Zang that morning to set up the breakfast meeting, so he could ease into asking for the favor. It wasn't like the task would be too difficult. He settled into his favorite corner booth with his PC and checked the daily news.

Ebola had hit Mali, but they were quarantining everyone. Please, like Africa could ever get it together. That continent was a hole and it would stay that way. He tapped the mouse pad. Anonymous brings down a jihadist site. Billy rolled his eyes and tapped the mouse pad again.

Fifteen minutes of cruel clicking passed. A man entered the café.

"Heya! You're new to these parts, what can I get ya?" Ms. Inappropriate practically screamed it at the newbie, but he ignored her and headed directly toward Billy.

He smiled warmly and took Billy's hand in a firm shake. His friend, Daniel Zang had been working with the NSA contracted to run the internet security division for just as long as Billy had been at his law firm.

Even though he was years older than Billy, the man hardly looked a day over 35. He was a slender, but fit man, and it showed in the well-tailored suits he wore. His hair was neat, cut short and jet black. Only the grayness at his temples betrayed his age.

Billy's order arrived just as Daniel took his seat. Daniel ordered himself a coffee latte to go. A couple seconds passed and Daniel checked his watch twice. Apparently, Zang hadn't allotted much time to a casual breakfast with a friend, so Billy cut right to it.

"I'm lucky to even be here right now. I was confronted by two men in the basement at work the other day."

The memory was enough to bring on a bad case of the goosebumps. He rubbed at the backs of his arms, over his coat, then slipped out of it and let it fall onto the vinyl seat behind him.

"Who were they?" Daniel rapped out a drum beat on the table, and glanced around. What was with him? So damn jumpy, it definitely wasn't his style.

"They left before I had a chance to find out. A couple of the other corporates came down for a meeting and it spooked them. I'll tell you, it's lucky that they did or I wouldn't be having this conversation with you." Billy tried for a jovial tone, but it came out strangled. There was something about impending doom which didn't amuse him, particularly when it was his impending doom at hand.

"What do you need?" Daniel accepted the latte, popped the lid, then tore open a Sweet'n Low and poured it into the cup. He used a wooden stick to stir it, tapped it three times, glanced over his shoulder and slapped the stick down on the table.

The ritual was something to behold. Billy used the moment to clear his thoughts and reorder them.

"I told you that I'm having some trouble at the company. Someone hacked my account, accessed information on CialCorp and sent off these spam emails. The head of the department said the spam was probably malware or something. So, all in all, I won't waste your time here. As I've told you, I'm really in a bind and it has our guy stumped, so I'm asking you to do a little digging for me."

"CialCorp," Daniel said, dark eyebrows climbing his forehead, caterpillars slinking on a pale pebble.

"You know them?" Billy chewed his thumbnail.

"I'm afraid you're in a world of trouble Billy. CialCorp has got their hands on some very sensitive technology which, in the wrong hands, could bring about a power shift like nothing we have seen before. But the real problem is that they are in bed with several terrorist organizations."

Billy pushed back against the seat, scrunching his coat in the small of his back. He didn't shift it out of the way.

"Whoa. All I want is my name cleared." He had the court hearing in a couple hours.

Daniel's face was stern and it made Billy uneasy. His friend kept that gaze and said in an even but low tone, "Don't move or say another word. There's a man sitting two tables away from us who's been here since I came in and hasn't ordered anything but that cup of coffee. He's been watching you this entire time. When I finish speaking, laugh as loudly as you can then hug me. I will meet you outside in the alleyway beside this café in 15 minutes. Don't be late."

Billy nodded stiffly then mustered up his best chuckle and did as he was told. Daniel had always been a fairly serious fellow but this side of him was new. He didn't think that anything he'd explained would illicit such a reaction. And CialCorp? Just what was that about?

"Am I tangled up in some terrorist plot? I cannot afford this kind of heat right now." Billy rambled it under his breath, barely paying attention to the breakfast bagel. He picked bits of cheese off. "Guess this means that Lorraine probably wasn't involved. Maybe I should apologize."

Like hell. He checked the time on the PC and considered how he'd waste 15 minutes. He'd opened a new Gmail account for correspondence during the investigation, so he opened it up, taking advantage of the restaurant's free Wi-Fi.

There was an update from Justin indicating he'd had no success pinpointing the source of the hack. However, he'd figured out that the feed would have come from overseas and the person had not only infiltrated his email, but had found a way to bypass the security system and access Whitland's personal files.

This was new information.

It was kind of flattering that he was important enough to be the target of corporate espionage. The next email came from an old client. An elderly lady named Mary whose husband had been the first big fish to give him a chance when he'd worked his way up the ranks.

Apparently, she'd been the victim of fraud, lost all of her liquid assets and she wasn't getting any satisfaction from the bank. He smiled to himself. This was just the kind of thing that made for great pro bono work and publicity. If the court hearing checked out and he got back on the case with CialCorp, he could swing this fraud case favorably. Then his acceptance into The Leather Lounge was guaranteed.

Billy gloated for a few minutes. If Daniel helped him out, he'd surely have clout in the hearing – the NSA working with him? They'd believe his story in a heartbeat. There was a light at the end of the tunnel. Billy looked up, saw the blond waitress and thought: "If that stupid concepts book is right, the light at the end of the tunnel doesn't necessarily mean a way out."

It was 8:30. Daniel had left 20 minutes ago. Billy hurriedly packed the club sandwich and laptop into his bag, then rushed out to meet Daniel in the alleyway. He couldn't resist glancing at the guy Daniel had mentioned. He was seated facing his booth and wore his cap low. Dark shades covered his eyes and he had on a long-sleeved denim jacket in an attempt to cover a sleeve of tattoos, which peered out beneath the cuffs.

There was a skull eating a snake on the back of his right hand.

Billy buried excitement – he could've been James Bond in this scenario – and jogged out of the café.

⁄⁄ ⁄⁄

Billy stood in the alley for half an hour, but there wasn't a trace of Daniel Zang.

He whipped out his smartphone and tapped through to his number, then dialed. He tried three times in a row, but the number kept cutting directly to voicemail.

Hi, you've reached Daniel Zang. Leave your name and number after the tone and I'll get back to you.

Bastard had stood Billy up. His hopes of presenting the NSA as his wildcard in the hearing dwindled. This was either Daniel's idea of a joke, or he didn't want to get involved in Billy's problems.

Why hadn't he just said so? Why lead him on with the whole 'bad guy watching him' act? Anger coiled around Billy's spine, mingling with the frustration of being taken for a ride by some overseas hacker with a penchant for lawyers.

It was too hot for this and the little alleyway carried the tang of urine and sour garbage. Tasty as that was, he had a hearing to attend, and the judge in his courthouse wasn't prone to waiting around.

This was his last chance to get into the Leather Lounge and make that name for himself.

It was nearing 9:00 and he had a meeting with the HR department at 9:30 this morning to make sure that Lorraine's dismissal was handled properly. He had to be on time for that, otherwise he'd send the wrong message. Besides, he didn't want to arrive bathed in his own sweat.

He made one more call to Daniel's phone as he strolled down the alleyway to get to his car. The voicemail cut in again.

"Hey man, been waiting for you for a while but it seems like you had to run. Sorry I was a little late but I've got some updated information for you. Give me a shout when you get this." He tucked the phone into his breast pocket and picked a path around a dirty diaper and the remains of a bucket of KFC Colonel's best.

There were legs sticking out from behind a dumpster further down the alleyway – most likely some drunkard who couldn't keep his life together. Idiot. Everyone in the world had a shot at life, and messing it up was inexcusable. Billy shook his head in disgust and put some pep in his step to deter the bum from asking him for anything.

He glanced in the person's direction and froze in place, foot suspended above a puddle of seeping filth. He stared into the dead eyes of Daniel Zang. Someone had shot him right in the middle of the forehead and posed his body like a passed out bum resting by a cardboard box.

Daniel's blood was the seeping filth. Flies buzzed around the scene. Bile climbed in Billy's throat. He turned away from the sight. The contents of his stomach worked up his throat.

"Don't move, kid." The guy in the low slung cap and jean shirt appeared ahead of him, and a man in a suit stepped out from behind the dumpster, polishing a pistol.

"I'm not involved in whatever this is, okay? I'm just a lawyer, a regular lawyer. I'm not with the government." Billy prattled it out, swiveling his head from one bad guy to the next.

"Oh, we know." The man raised the pistol and shot him once

in each leg. Billy collapsed to the ground, numbness spread around the wounds.

He looked down. Blood pumped through his pants. The pain came in searing waves, scouring his mind clean.

He keeled over and fell into the puddle of Daniel's blood, except it smelled strange. Sickly sweet and not coppery at all.

Billy stared at Daniel, laid against the wall, bathing in the agony and trying to think. Trying to figure out what to do. He couldn't run.

The man's black shoes walked up to him. He cocked the gun.

Bang!

Blackness.

CHAPTER 14

The morning sun broke through the curtains and lit her face. She'd been awake for hours already, staring at the ceiling. Today was the day. She'd chosen to go back to school and face the music.

Hailey sighed and swallowed a few times. There'd be a reckoning when she got into the halls. There'd be jokes. People would probably throw stuff again. Man, she just didn't want to hurl chunks like last time. She rolled over onto her stomach and breathed through her nose.

"Please, God, if you're up there, please let today go well. Please, give me the strength to get through this." Hailey scrunched her eyes up tight and pleaded. The flowery pillowcase her mom had bought her last year was wet with tears. She gave a few sobs to get them out of her system, then cleared her throat.

She had to do this. Maria would be there. She'd sent a stream of incriminating messages in the past weeks, but Hailey had ignored them. She'd kept them in case there was a court case, but otherwise she'd avoided reading them altogether.

Hailey sat up and scrubbed at her cheeks. This was weird. There were no blog posts to write, no tweets or Facebook status updates. She'd cut herself off from social media completely, deleted all her accounts – even the Evernote app on her smartphone.

She couldn't allow for the off chance that somebody would find a way to torment her again.

The whole affair had finally blown over – at least a little.

Hailey went to her dresser and pulled out a plain pair of jeans and a pink blouse she'd gotten for her birthday. She paired them up, then put on the silver bracelet mom and dad had bought her after she'd made straight A's for the second year running. She'd find a college which would take her. She would! It was only a matter of time.

Today, she'd need all the luck she could get.

Hailey ambled downstairs and tucked her phone into her pocket. Her parents had already left for work, but mom had left a plate of pancakes for her with a tiny pitcher of maple syrup.

She warmed them up and poured the syrup over, then sat down and tried to get them in. She chewed the cud, forcing the delicious breakfast down, but tasting dust instead of sweetness.

Everything was different. Everything smelled, looked and tasted different and Hailey hadn't had real fun in ages.

She sighed and searched around for the TV remote. Maybe there'd be something on to distract her from the drama.

Beep, beep.

The message tone on her phone went off and she checked it. Maria again. She didn't read the message.

Beep, beep.

Another message. Then another, and another. Her phone went crazy, beeping nonstop for two minutes straight. There was a gap of 30 seconds, then more messages came through.

What the hell was this about?

She turned the phone over in her hands, and cleared her notifications, then put it on silent. The kids had obviously found out she'd come back to school that morning, and wanted to get in a few jibes early.

It was ridiculous. Nausea and anger combined in her stomach and mixed the pancakes around. Hailey clapped a hand to her mouth and kept it down. Barely.

She left the phone on the countertop and hurried to the front hall. She picked up her backpack and squared her shoulders.

The doorbell rang and she frowned. Who could that be? Hopefully, not a few high school kids come to start the torture early. She walked the three steps to the door, took a breath and opened up.

"Hailey, we are live on the *You'll Be The Judge show* with Sarah Mcdaniel and we want to give you an opportunity to tell us your side of the story. What comments do you have about the videos circulating, right now?" There was a woman on the front porch with a microphone in front of Hailey's face, catty-corner from the reporter there was a man toting a video camera.

"Was it consensual sex or were you drugged?" The skinny woman, in a navy blue pants suit, asked.

"Are you being bullied at school?"

Hailey stared for a few seconds, but the slew of questions carried on and the reporter wasn't the only one there. There were some schoolmates taking selfies in front of her house. It was a nightmare of reality TV proportions and she couldn't escape.

They'd plucked her out of nowhere and slammed her down in the middle of this.

She hadn't asked for it.

"Hailey? When did you first realize you were a sex addict?"

"What do your parents think of all this?"

"Are you receiving psychological care?" The questions continued, filling her head with a low buzz of anxiety. She stumbled back and slammed the door, then locked it.

"This can't be happening."

There wasn't a chance a local news station had that much interest in her story She stumbled through to the kitchen, the tiles swayed up to meet her, but she grabbed onto the island in the middle of the room and held herself up.

The remote was on top of the microwave. She picked it up and flicked on the TV.

CNN was on.

"Live from Los Angeles, California, I am your host Sarah Mcdaniel and with me is child protective services, David Mahon. Here we just present the facts and *You'll Be The Judge*. Today we are looking at teen choices. But this isn't the Teen Choice Awards. This is serious business and the question of the day is: Is this a case of teen promiscuity or online bullying? You'll be the judge." The horrid reporter wiggled her eyebrows, then continued, "In a moment we'll ask one of the most infamous (or famous) young women in America to defend her actions. We're broadcasting live so we have no idea what will happen. Stay tuned."

Sarah Mcdaniel turned to David Mahon and asked, "In the news we have a teenager posting pictures of herself online. Most of them in incredibly compromising positions with men, in what appears to be an orgy setup. What in the world would drive someone to do that?"

Tufts of hair surrounded David Mahon's bald crown. He pushed a pair of glasses up a sweaty hooked nose.

Hailey fell into a chair.

"Hi, Sarah, and thanks for having me. I believe this kind of behavior shows an alarming disregard for safety. This teen is clearly disrespecting herself, her family and her educators. It's abhorrent and a clear reflection of where our youth is headed." David shook his head and pursed his lips. Sarah nodded along with his words.

"There are several pictures posted on her blog. And it seems she's more bragging about this than anything else." Sarah scratched her chin with the tip of a long, red nail, then retrieved a few papers from an assistant off camera. "This is a quote from her latest post which was uploaded in conjunction with the pictures 'Had an amazing time with these fellas. Call me, guys and we'll give it another go.' The rest is too explicit to read on air, but you get the gist."

Hailey gasped for air and lowered her head onto the counter. David Mahon's rebuttal faded into white noise.

It was clear now. This was her life. She wouldn't escape this and no one would believe her side of the story. Her parents didn't have money to fight this legally, not something this big.

Hailey would carry this with her until the day she died.

Her life was over.

No college. No success. No jobs. No guy would want her after this.

Her mind cleared, focusing on that single point and multiplying by millions, billions even.

Whispers told her, 'Her life was over.'

Hailey breathed in through her nose and pushed herself up from the chair. The dull knocking and scraping on the front door spurred her on. She walked through the house and let herself into the garage attached to the side of the house.

Her father's car wasn't there and the garage door was shut tight. She moved to his workbench and picked up the coil of rope he'd used to build her a swing when she was a kid. He'd taken it down last summer because she didn't use it anymore.

The sycamore tree out front had looked empty after that.

Hailey tucked it under arm and went back into the house. She traipsed up the stairs and tied one end of the rope to the top balustrade. She could just make out the outlines of the news van on the front lawn through the misted glass of the window.

She tied the other end around her neck and climbed over the wooden banister. It should hold. The last thing she wanted was to break her legs instead.

Hailey filled her lungs with air.

She was five and her father was clapping his hands behind her, smiling and laughing. She was on her new cherry red bike. Flash. Mom's apple pie on her 10 birthday. Flash. Maria joking with her about Gino. Flash. Mom and dad at dinner, holding hands and smiling back at her.

Then pain.

She envisioned herself leaping. There was a snap. Blackness.

The doorbell rang again. Hailey went from sadness to fury in a heartbeat. She dropped the rope and ran to the door to let them have a piece of her mind before the end. She opened the door, but there was no one there, except for the middle school boy who lived around the corner.

He was a bit of a dweeb really. "What do you want?" Hailey yelled.

"Did you know that God loves you? He came to the world to save you." The statement took Hailey by surprise; the concept that someone loved her in the midst of all that she'd experienced – it filled her with warmth for a moment.

"What's your name?" Hailey asked.

"Doug," the boy replied.

"Thanks for stopping by, Doug, but I'm busy. Gotta go," Hailey said, she swung the door to close it.

Doug placed his palm on the wood panels to stop its path. "Wait! Give me a few minutes and I can prove it to you."

"Prove what?" asked Hailey.

"That God really loves you and he wants to be your friend and he wants to take all your troubles away." Doug replied. "Can I come in? Give me 10 minutes. That's all."

Hailey looked at him. He was so bold to do this, and she kinda admired that. Realization sank into her soul: earlier she'd asked God for help. Maybe he'd listened.

She invited Doug in and he sat on the sofa with her. He explained the amazing sacrifice which Jesus made when He took away all sins, past, present and future. Hailey believed, and in that very moment it was as if a first-class warm towel had embraced her.

The healing of the one true God settled over her, and just like that, she was a new person. The old was gone and a happiness she had never experienced settled in her heart.

Hailey didn't go to school that day, she started to read the Bible and it wasn't just a book of stories, there was deep meaning behind it. Time flew by and her mother came home and saw the noosed rope on the banister. She crashed into Hailey's bedroom upstairs and found her reading the Bible.

"What happened?"

"It was amazing, Mom, I was so afraid and the Lord came to me. Well, actually, it was the next door neighbor, but he told me the most amazing things."

"You were afraid?" Her mother asked, gripping the door handle.

"Yes, I saw what they were saying on the TV, and I wanted to end it, for good, but then –"

"What are they saying on the TV?" Her mother asked, eyes widening, but she didn't stay for the answer. She stormed downstairs and CNN blared to life. "NO!" Her mother's shriek echoed up the stairs.

Hailey didn't pay attention to the muffled judgments of the reporters, or David Mahon, or anyone else. Instead, she hunched over her new favorite book, and kept reading.

CHAPTER 15

"I don't care how you do it, Davoli, but you'd better find her again." His boss was in the middle of an aneurism about Jia. He huffed and puffed, and Greg could picture his purpling complexion. He'd seen this reaction one too many times with the other agents.

Greg Davoli had never been on the receiving end, he was a star on the force, but hell, there was a first time for everything, right?

He held the note and brushed the words 'I'm sorry' with the tips of his fingers. "I'll get her back," he promised, more to himself than to the boss man.

"You'd better damn well, or you can kiss a promotion goodbye. In fact, you can pretty much count on a demotion at this rate." Carlos growled and there was the telltale click of the lighter on the other end of the phone. His boss inhaled and exhaled, and Greg envisioned the curling smoke, brushing past his nostrils and into the space above his head. "What were you thinking, Greg? This isn't like you at all." Carlos lowered his voice and the anger turned to concern.

"I've been confused lately." He didn't say about what.

"About what?"

What could he say? Confused about the job, about his existence, about the purpose of his life? His niece was a subject of social estrangement and there was nothing he could do to change that. The world was muddy, and the one person who seemed to have it figured out to any extent was the person he had to capture and subject to the rules he'd loved and lived by, but which seemed false to him.

Greg Davoli, the hard-working agent, had disappeared, replaced by Greg Davoli, the man who couldn't think straight because of a college grad with a sweet smile and an attitude which could set the world on fire.

"Davoli?" Carlos hummed with impatience.

"It doesn't matter, Boss. I'll get it done."

Carlos heaved a sigh. "Make sure you do, because I can't take any more of the heat from the big guys. They're breathing down my neck every other second. It's like having central heating in my office. Make it happen."

"You got it."

Carlos clicked off the line before he got the words out. That was that. Get back the girl or he was out for a better position, better pay.

The question was: did he even want that? He ruffled his hair and made a low growl. He crumpled the note into a paper ball and lobbed it at the tiny TV.

He'd worked hard for this life and now he didn't even want it. Jia had walked in and aggravated the issues he'd had, showed him there was more than grunt work. Life was more than grinding yourself to the bone without any purpose.

He wanted freedom. He wanted purpose.

He wanted …

He cleared his throat. She was in Washington.

His phone rang and his pulse quickened.

Greg clicked the green button and lifted it to his ear. "Hello?"

"Greg," his sister cried. "Greg, is that you?"

"Rose, what's wrong?" Fingers of terror felt their way up his spine, gripping at his flesh until they pinched the base of his neck. "What is it? Is Hailey okay?"

"Hailey," Rose shrieked it over the phone, then dissolved into wordless sobs.

Greg stood and paced back and forth, glaring at the wall – it was empty of decoration. "Slow down. What's happened?"

Rose blubbered incoherently for another two minutes but Greg didn't push her. She'd speak when she was ready. That was an interrogation technique, not to mention common courtesy: the silence got to everyone in the end.

"Hailey tried to commit suicide."

Greg buckled inside, but the FBI training kept him upright, frozen to the spot. "How?"

"She tried to hang herself," Rose wept into the receiver, leaking agony and pain through to Greg. It infected his spirit and dulled his anger at Carlos, at Jia, at the situation in general.

"Because of the pictures?" It was something Hailey would've

stood up to. This didn't make sense.

"It was all over her blog, Facebook, Twitter. The entire internet and then someone saw them and," Rose swallowed, the tears disappeared, replaced by mournful anger. She continued, "Turn on your TV. Watch CNN."

Greg jabbed the button on the front of the TV and an image appeared. It was CNN, and Hailey's name and face were plastered all over the screen.

Promiscuous teen or victim of cyberbullying?

The title offended him to his core.

"She was obviously mentally unstable, judging from the progression from nude photographs, complete transparency about it on social media and then the attempt on taking her own life. I suggest the police look into drug use on this one." It was a psychologist, or some bookish type in the hot seat.

No, in the cool studio, giving his opinion about Greg's niece as if he'd known her. As if he cared.

"Rose, I'll come to you. I'll come talk to her."

"It's done already, Greg. I'm sorry." Rose's voice was hollow.

"I'm so sorry, Sissy. I wish I could be there for you," he whispered, cracking under the strain of this revelation. He punched the button on the TV and the image of his niece winked out.

"Greg," she muttered, "What do I do? What do I do, now? My baby's reputation is gone."

"I – I don't know, Sissy."

The line went dead.

Greg dropped the phone onto the table, then slammed his fist through the window. Shards of glass splintered off in every direction and he pulled his hand back to nurse the cuts.

He went to his bag and pulled out his medic kit, then applied bandages and salve.

Jia was right: the world was on fire. The scum of humanity seethed around them and social media was their new platform. A weapon used against good people, innocents like Hailey.

She'd had such a bright future. She'd been the light of the family.

Greg finished up and swung the bag over his shoulder, then collected his phone from the desk. He brushed bits of glass from its screen and tucked it into his jeans.

Greg slammed the door behind him on the way out.

This was it. He had to find Jia.

But not to bring her back, to join her.

CHAPTER 16

"How about some champagne?" Jia asked, with a grin and one hand on that white anonymous mask. She kept it close by out of habit, as motivation and a reminder of what was wrong with the world.

And how she'd fix it.

"No time for that now," Debra muttered, hunched over the keyboard and typing furiously. The tap of the keys was a melody to Jia, now, she was so accustomed to it. She could sway in time to the rhythm and hum a tune.

She wouldn't though, because Debra would lose her mind and throw an eraser at her. She knew this from experience.

They'd already taken Twitter down with multiple concurrent Denial Of Service and keeping it that way was Anonymous' first priority. Jia's first priority was to scrape Facebook from the face of the internet. She had a personal vendetta against it now.

"We're going to do it." Debra gritted her teeth, the lines of code reflected in her fierce expression. "We have to."

"Of course we're going to.do it. There's no other option, Deb. This is the way the world is meant to be, not some pseudo global country where everyone knows everything all the time. It's like we're handing the power to the wrong dudes." Jia got on a roll, swaying in her chair and bopping her head on every other syllable.

"You're preaching to the choir," Debra answered with a sigh. She was so focused, she never took a break. Jia hardly recognized her anymore. Her hair was pulled back tight and her lips were drawn into a thin line.

Debra had committed herself to the cause for her own sweet vengeance. She wanted Taylor's name cleared.

The Coppell housewife was gone. The student was gone. Debra was a shell of her former self and she was possessed by the need to make things right.

"Mommy?" Shannon appeared in the doorway in her pink-patterned nightgown.

"What is it Sweetheart?" Debra asked, through her clenched jaw and Jia tensed up. She'd barely had parents growing up in the U.S. and she hated the thought that this would claim Debra's relationship with the kid.

"Can I have a hug, Mommy? I had a nightmare."

"I'm a little busy now, Sweetheart."

They were doing the right thing, weren't they? What would Greg have called it? Cyber-terrorism. It wasn't like they'd hurt anybody. This was the only way to shut down the sludge of human crap online.

Things had probably been better in the 50s. She studied Shannon, and her heart did a motherly tha-thump.

"Deb," Jia put in, before the girl's chin did the tell-tale pre-cry wobble, "Take a break. Go be with Shannon for a bit. I'll manage here, okay?"

Taking down Facebook by herself? Hell yes! She'd go down in the legends for that one. Anonymously, of course. Wait, that didn't work. She frowned and scratched at her temple with a the rubber end of her pencil.

"Thanks, Jia," Debra seemed reluctant to go, but she rose out of her chair and herded Shannon out of the room regardless. "Come on, Love. Everything will be all right."

"I'm sure he's not dead, Mommy. I'm sure." Shannon whispered back and goosebumps sprang up on the back of Jia's neck. The kid was weird, older inside than she was on the outside.

No time for that now, she had to get to work on Facebook. She cracked her neck, punched the air a couple times, then twiddled her fingers and lowered them to the keyboard.

She typed in silence for a few minutes and sweat sprang up on her forehead. She swept it away with the back of her hand and continued. This site had insane protection. She faced a chain-link fence the size of the Empire State, with a pair of scissors to cut through it.

The door squeaked open behind her, but she didn't bother looking over her shoulder.

"Deb, I told you to take a break. You can't just work until you shatter."

"You can say that again," a male voice spoke up behind her.

"What the –" She spun in her chair and gasped. It was Greg. "What are you doing here?"

"I came to find you," he said, taking a step toward her. If he got too close, her resolve might melt. She couldn't allow that.

"Hold it, Buddy," Jia said and jumped up to stop him. "I don't know what you thought you'd achieve by coming here, but I'm not going anywhere. Do you understand me?"

"Who said you had to go anywhere?" Greg drew closer and Jia's chest constricted. She wanted to be around him – she'd missed him even though she didn't want to – but it wasn't possible. He would do what was right for the 'Country'.

"What do you mean, Davoli?"

"I've decided I like it when you call me that. And I mean you can stay here, I haven't come to take you away, Jia."

"Not that you could if you wanted to," Jia answered, stubborn as a mule, "but why not? Aren't you supposed to be licking boots right now?"

"Aw, that's so sweet, Darling. I missed you, too."

"Come on, I didn't mean it like that."

"I'm not here to take you away, Jia, I'm here to join you," Greg said, calm as he'd ever been. Like he hadn't just announced he'd done a total philosophical 180.

"What? When? Ho – "

"My niece almost killed herself." Greg blurted it out, then reached up and loosened his collar slightly. "Sorry, I'm a little wound up."

"Oh my God, Greg. What happened?"

"Social media happened. A plague of scumbags happened.

You were right, Jia, and I'm not going to stand by and let it happen anymore. I'm here to help."

"Okay, okay," she said, waving him into the chair, then kneeling beside him. He met her gaze and cupped her chin with one hand.

"I also wanted to see you again."

"I'm sorry for the way I left things, Greg, but I couldn't stay. I was sure you'd turn me in. I understand, it's your job."

"Not anymore." He brushed a line down the edge of her jaw and it set her nerves tingling.

"What? You quit?"

"Not in so many words. But they'll get the picture when I don't show up in a couple weeks."

"Greg, are you sure about this?" What if it was the wrong thing to do and she'd dragged him down into it?

He drew her into his lap and gave her a soft kiss. "I've never been surer of anything in my life."

She sighed and melted into him for a moment, melding with his chest and breathing alongside him. "What really happened?"

"Some kids took pictures of her. They drugged her and implicated her in an orgy, then they spread it all over the net. People assumed she was looking for attention and half-crazed and there's nothing anyone can do to convince them otherwise. Her reputation is gone forever and my sister, God, she's a wreck. I don't want that to happen to anyone else, Jia."

"We won't let it happen." Jia answered and patted his torso. "I just have to figure out a way to get you into Anonymous without them having a fit. After all they're not likely to trust a Fed, ya know."

"That's fine. But Jia, we still need to take the Gang of 8 down. The sooner we clear your name, the sooner we're free to do whatever we want."

The fact he'd used 'we' touched her in the romantic places in her soul. She was too mushy these days!

"Don't worry, we'll handle them and every other scumbag out there."

"Good, because –"

"What's this?" Debra stood in the doorway with several of the other Anonymous members behind her. They eyed Greg, the fresh meat and them the butchers.

"Debra, this is Greg Davoli."

"Oh, we know who he is. We keep tabs on the FBI too, you know." She strolled into the room, her expression all hard panes and angles.

"Wait a minute, give me a chance to explain," Greg said, and Jia hopped out of his lap. He rose and the Anonymous members spread out in a semi-circle.

"There's no explanation needed. You're leaving. Now." Debra clicked her fingers and one of the members – a burly guy with a thicket of chest hair – moved forward, cracking his knuckles.

Greg gave a grin and shrugged Jia off his arm.

"Or what?"

CHAPTER 17

This was the worst thing which could've happened to Jeff.

Anand secreted his smile and kept his eyes glued to his laptop screen, feigning interest in the rows of data. He surveyed the room – the rest of the suits in the conference room were too preoccupied with the 'crisis' to notice the farce.

This was a gathering of the most powerful criminals in the country, flown from the corners of the U.S. for Jeff's big screw up.

The Misters were all in attendance in varying degrees of age and baldness, and three of the top lawyers from the Blackwater Group sat at the end of the table.

"This is not going to be an easy fight." A stern lawyer with a red velvet tie, glared around at the others. "We'll need access to a lot of resources if you want to cover it up."

'Resources' meant a lot of money and nothing was off-limits. That was what the grand America had boiled down to: capitalism and greed. Better to rid the world of that belief before it ruined more lives.

Mr. 2 glanced at Jeff and a flicker of a snarl spread across his lips. "Oh, we'll find those resources somewhere. What's important now, is fixing this mess before it's too late. Before the FBI, CIA and all the rest come down on our behinds."

Jeff was at the bottom of the totem pole in the gang. He'd been allotted the low-level work in the business. He dealt with the prostitution and sex trafficking initiatives, identity theft scams, as well as the low-level investment and pension rackets. But Jeff had grown tired of the lot he'd been provided.

He'd dabbled in some of the high-level schemes – on Anand's prodding, of course – that were usually handled by others. It was unheard of in the Gang. Retribution would be swift for Jeff – Anand was just a lesser, unimportant in their eyes.

"Mr. Aceves, it seems that there is almost no way to completely avoid any thorough investigation unless we manage to completely sever any connection that would tie you to the situation. However, as your partner has informed us that the issue is with some overlap between your … umm," he cleared his throat in a familiar manner. "… your different business initiatives, this would put a lot of pressure on any legal team representing you. Can you explain to us what really happened?"

This was it. Anand grinned and closed the laptop lid, though no one gave him a second glance. That suited him. These fools in their suits with their billions were puny in comparison to him. If they knew the power he wielded, or would wield in good time, they'd grovel before him.

Instead, he was the 'partner,' the assistant who was below notice.

Jeff passed his hand over his head and said:

"In a nutshell, my investment schemes with the pensioners got caught up with our plan to get information on CialCorp's IPO because some old biddy happened to know the lawyer handling the IPO. So when she reached out to him about her problem, then she made herself a person of interest in his murder. We got some of her information via an internet ad campaign where she signed-up for our consultant services on short-term investments." He paused and met Anand's gaze, but the man simply nodded encouragement. Jeff would walk on alone in this.

Aceves clapped his hands together and rubbed them. "Then we used the cookies in her browser to access her actual computer for any additional information. So, any IT specialist worth his salt can probably find traces of us having been in her system unless we can find a way to either cut it off or have the consultancy firm pay her off and hope that curbs the investigation. In either case, we still have to deal with any repercussions from our actual hacking of Mr. Whitland's work emails. The NSA does not employ your run of the mill office IT guys so we must act quickly and nip this in the bud."

He inhaled deeply at the end of his little speech. He'd hardly taken a breath through it, and was shaken to the core. It made Anand settle back.

They weren't just business partners. Anand was the backbone of all of his cyber operations and a trusted confidante. Jeff was nothing without him, but Anand was everything without Jeff. Not that Aceves knew it, of course.

"And who gave you the go ahead to go after CialCorp's IPO? Insider trading is not your M.O. Mr. 8." Seven said it in a way which meant Aceves wouldn't be a number for much longer.

That wouldn't be a huge problem anymore, Anand had just about achieved what he'd needed to, though the missing data on CialCorp was a bit of a worry.

"It was an executive decision. I figured it would generate more money, a better rep. You know how it goes," Jeff pleaded.

"And the fact that CialCorp has an algorithm which could give you all the information on every technological consumer in the country makes no nevermind to you?" One seldom spoke, but when he did, the other men fell quiet and bowed their heads a little.

"It crossed my mind," Jeff half-squeaked.

"Mr. Aceves, the ramifications of your actions are dire for us. If the NSA ties Billy Whitland to you, and you to us, you can bet that the retribution will be swift and terminal."

The retribution was in reference to that acted out by the gang. Anand sighed. He had work to do, people to track. Daniel Zang had disappeared and if the rumors were true, he was killed in that alley with Whitland, then Anand was home free.

Just about clear to walk right into CialCorp and take what he wanted right from under their noses.

Jeff stuttered, "We can fix this, right?"

Anand got up and left the room. Jeff would likely need him at some point, but he didn't care. He strolled downstairs to check out the progress of his exploits. Conveniently, he had set-up an automated feed that was regularly dumped into one of his Jia Kailai's Twitter accounts – he had Jia's account up.

He entered in the URL, but a blank page came up. Error 404. Page Not Found.

"What the hell?"

Twitter was down. No, it wasn't even down, it was gone completely.

A low thrill of alarm ran up and down his spine. There was something wrong. He typed in Twitter's IP address, but nothing. Then he flitted off to some of his favorite underground news sites in search for anyone bragging about taking down Twitter. There was nothing in the news, but an alert showed next to his profile image.

He clicked through to his profile and a white mask popped up on the screen.

It was the signature of movement. The white anonymous mask.

Anand's heart went cold. He read the blinking message beneath the face.

You're Next.

A hand clamped down on his shoulder.

"Mr. Vermugante?"

Anand shrugged the hand from his shoulder and slapped his laptop shut. "What the hell do you want?"

He swivelled in the chair and stared down the blonde assistant. She was curvy in the right places, her shirt stretched across her chest, and she'd popped the collar and unbuttoned it to reveal more cleavage.

That was her way to present herself and get what she wanted.

She was likely on her way to the top by being on the bottom, but Anand didn't have time for lowly tramps.

"I'm sorry to interrupt you, sir," she said, batting her eyelids which were coated in a thin layer of glitter, "but Mr. Aceves has requested your presence upstairs."

"Yeah, thanks." Anand made to turn back to his laptop, but the blonde chick didn't move off at his dismissal. "Was there something else?"

"Oh, sorry, I-I'm meant to escort you upstairs myself." The assistant gestured back to the bank of elevators with a vapid smile, and swayed her hips from side-to-side. She wore a tight black skirt to complete her outfit.

Anand stood and tucked the laptop under his arm. "You're meant to escort me." He chuckled. "While I'm sure you have the experience in 'escorting,' I'm sure I'll be able to find the conference room by myself."

"I'm afraid I'm going to have to insist, Anand," she answered, and stopped swaying to cock her hip and fold her arms. This was the one Jeff had hand-picked for the job and it was obvious why. She was eye candy and nothing else.

There was fluff between the ears.

"And I'm going to insist that you leave before I contact your superior and have you fired for insubordination." He said it with the calm ease which didn't match the roiling fury in his stomach.

This twit thought she could order him around? He was practically her boss.

Her baby blues went round as dinner plates. "Yes, but –"

"Get lost, kid." He barked and the blonde girl jumped, fluffed her hair and hurried away, glancing back over her shoulder every few steps, scandalized by his rough treatment.

Perfect. She'd likely hurry back upstairs and tell Jeff that he'd molested her or something. He didn't have time to entertain Jeff or his bimbos, or the puny Gang of 8 for that matter.

They didn't appreciate his power, his skill, so he didn't have time to do anything other than crush them.

This Twitter thing was a worry, however.

Anand strolled to the exit, past the glass sliding doors, and out into the city. He summoned a taxi with a practiced whistle and ordered the driver to take him to his favorite coffee place.

He glared out at the skyscrapers and rubbed the bridge of his nose.

Years had passed since he'd lived on the streets of Mumbai. Less since his mother had sold him to an American couple with big plans for their adoptive son. And now, Anand was where he'd always wanted to be.

Or moments from it at least.

He paid the taxicab driver and rushed into the café. His phone beeped, but he ignored it and settled into one of the booths. There was free fiber optics WiFi at least, but the annoying waitress took too long with his cappuccino and the buzz of the other patrons irritated him to no end.

It was better than Paradigm, though.

Anand opened the laptop and considered Twitter for a moment. The ominous warning on his profile in the hacker's chat room had unsettled him.

He clicked through to the online file – encrypted of course – which he'd shared with Jeff. It contained their recovered info on CialCorp and the key to getting their hands on the algorithm that would make sense of any amount of Big Data a thing of the present. He had nicknamed it The Scrapper because of its ability to crunch zettabytes of data in picoseconds from every U.S. citizen and predict just about every move and choices any single person could make.

With that kind of information power, the Islamic State could control or wipe the West from the face of the planet.

He typed in the password to the folder and it opened up. Anand's extremities turned to ice. That freeze spread up his arms and into his chest, circling around his rib cage and squeezing the air out of his lungs.

Anand leaned forward and wheezed. "What?"

It was empty. The information was gone. Countless hours of hacking, probing and recon on CialCorp ... wasted. It was gone.

Anand grimaced. His external hard drive was back at Paradigm, and on it were his backups of the information. His phone let off another series of beeps and he finally pulled it out to check.

Texts from Jeff.

Where are you?

Anand rolled his eyes and deleted the message, then clicked through to the next one.

The Gang of 8 has taken insider trading away from me. Nothing I can do, Anand. I need you to convince them otherwise.

The messages went from confusion to panic in a blink.

They've taken the information on CialCorp. The IPO info, the data. It's gone. Files have been wiped.

He texted back: ***Have extra data on my external. Backups. We're still okay.***

Then he took several breaths to calm his stomach and drank from the coffee. It was water in the oasis, though the cappuccino was more of an Americano than anything else. The barista was as much of a moron as the assistant.

He'd down it, sneak upstairs and get his external hard drive, then hightail it out of there before the Gang of 8 or Aceves got wind of his presence.

His message tone bleeped again.

They got it.

A sharp spine of pure anger drove through Anand's chest.

He'd lost everything.

Actually, Jeff had lost everything with his foolish insistence on the pensioner scheme. He'd dabbled in the cheap stuff for too long and he'd demanded they look into Mary's accounts.

Jeff Aceves had effectively ruined Anand's plan in one foul swoop. He'd have to find another way to get to CialCorp, because buying the shares and overpowering the company wasn't an option anymore.

"Do you want anything else?" The waitress leaned against the table and chewed on gum.

"No." He snapped it out and dismissed her with a wave.

There was nothing left for him to do but find a way in. But first, he had a hacker to attend to. The white anonymous face mask was too familiar.

Five minutes later, he drew in a breath and retracted from the cyberworld.

Anonymous was on the move, and they were taking down social media sites.

He dove back into the underbelly of the internet, burying himself in information, searching for the answer. Who was it? Who had come after his profile?

Who had tracked him?

Anand gasped. Jia Kailai. He rubbed his eyes beneath his round glasses and glared at the screen. This witch was on his case. She'd discovered him somehow, maybe even the fake Facebook account, and she thought she could take him down?

It was laughable.

Anand had been in this business too long to see it fall around his ears thanks to an upstart IT Tech with a bone to pick.

She wanted trouble? She'd damn well get it.

CHAPTER 18

Jia chewed her lip and stared at the computer screen. It'd been days since they'd accepted Greg into their midst, but things were far from done.

Facebook was up and functional.

She'd achieved a small triumph by hacking into her fake Jia profile, copying across all the transcripts of messages, then deleting it. Taking down the whole thing, however, was a challenge she couldn't quite crack.

"I can barely keep my eyes open," Debra said, though it came out garbled behind a yawn. It was past 3 a.m. and they'd been at it for six hours straight.

Six hours of tracking down Islamic State operatives, shutting down government sites, shutting down social media sites. It was six hours of breaking down society.

Jia swallowed. This was what she'd become – was this right? Would breaking it down help? And who would build it up again?

"Jia? Are you okay?" Debra had softened a little, but there was an ingrained drive in the wriggle of her fingers over the keyboard.

"I'm fine. Just exhausted and frustrated. I don't know how long it'll take before we break through here."

"We'll get it done, we just have to keep going until it's down. Look at Twitter." Debra gave a grin, then stood slowly.

They'd obliterated the social network. The site wasn't just down, it was gone, erased from the server.

"I've got to get some sleep," Debra said, but with that reluctant shrug of her shoulders. She'd be up at 6 again to read to Shannon and fix her food. Debra had taken her daughter's education upon herself. "Are you coming?"

"Nah, I think I'll try a while longer. Catch you lataz." Jia turned back to the screen and squished around in the chair. She stretched her neck and considered her empty mug of coffee on the corner of the desk.

There was movement behind her and she jumped, but Greg placed a hand on the back of her neck and calmed her. He leaned in and kissed her on the shoulder.

"You're up late."

"Yeah, I'm kind of busy." Jia grunted it. Greg had been great to have around for her sake, but he hadn't contributed as much to the cause as she'd have liked.

"What are you up to?" He pulled a chair up and settled in beside her, still resting his palm against her neck. Any other time it would have soothed, but not tonight.

"Trying to take down Facebook. I swear, it's locked up tighter than a gnat's wallet. You've got to take a look at this. Maybe you can lend an experienced eye to this stuff." Who knew what they taught the agents in the FBI.

"I think I'll take a rain check on that."

"What? Why?" Jia's brow wrinkled and she stroked at the furrows self-consciously. She'd be old before her years at this rate.

"Because Jia, taking down Facebook isn't the answer. If I could stop you from doing it I would, but I figure it would be easier to stop a raging bull than it would be to stop you."

He was right there.

"Are you crazy? What about Hailey? What about how social media destroys lives?" Jia swivelled in her chair and leaned back to study his expression.

"For sure. Social media is a devil, but it's one humanity created and erasing it won't achieve much. You can chop the head off the snake, but soon enough another one will crop up."

"Another head?"

"Another snake."

"So, what, we should just give up while we're ahead?" Jia puffed her cheeks out then let the air whistle past her lips. "Wow, of all the people I thought would understand this and want to help, it would be you."

"I'm angry about Hailey. Social media is wrong and depraved, but –"

"How can there be a 'but' to that? If it's depraved, it has to go." Jia was a fan of logic, but the doubt eating at the lining of her stomach disturbed her.

"Anonymous is wrong to do it this way. Brute force won't win the war."

"What way do you suggest then, Davoli? Since you follow the God of reason and justice."

"Stop overreacting for five seconds and just listen to what I'm saying." He touched her arm, stroking the bare skin below her blouse, but she flinched away.

"Then start making sense." Jia's answer dripped acid.

"Breaking down society as we know it, won't stop the tide of filth. You're debasing yourself to their level by trying. Anonymous isn't saving the world from itself, it's terrorizing them. This is cyber warfare, no, cyber terrorism at its finest and I'm surprised you want to be a part of it."

Jia slapped the desk and the coffee mug fell off and shattered on the tiles, splatting brown fluid on his loafers.

"I'm surprised you don't want to be a part of it, after that speech you gave me a few days ago. Or was that a lie so that you could get in with us?"

"Don't be ridiculous."

"Infiltrating so you can take me back to your boss and get your raise or promotion or whatever."

"Stop, Jia, that's enough," he barked it. Davoli never lost his temper – she'd clearly touched a nerve.

"So, why did you join then? For me? Cos I gotta tell you, Babe, that's kinda pathetic."

"I joined because I thought it was a cause I could lend myself to. I want social media gone, but I didn't think it would happen like this. Erasing entire sites? I mean, come on, don't you see what kind of toll that will take on the world?"

"Same toll it took on your niece?"

"Watch it," he warned, raising a finger, and she snorted at him. "Think of how many businesses advertise on there. How many people rely on it, good people?"

"A few corporates get shafted? Big deal. Sounds like a bonus to me." But the sinking feeling in Jia's gut said otherwise.

"Not corporates. Small businesses, friends, families. There are folks across the world communicating on these platforms. If you break it all down, you'll have nothing left to work with. What don't you get?"

"If this is all you have to contribute, then get out. I don't need you here."

Greg slumped slightly and reached for her again, but she scraped away from him.

"I mean it. Get out of here. I don't need your judgment."

She'd lost everything because of the FBI and the Gang of 8. He didn't understand her need for vengeance. Her life was in ruins!

"You don't mean that, Jia." Greg's voice rumbled in his chest.

"Read my lips. Get. Out." She pointed to the door and turned back to the computer, then poked at the keys with such force that the keyboard rattled against the wood of the desk.

Greg walked past her, boots crunching on the shards of the broken cup.

Jia sat for two minutes glaring into space, but that gut-wrenching sadness didn't leave her.

He was right. And she couldn't let him leave if he had the means to make it better somehow.

She bolted out of the chair and through the building up the stairs, through the doors and out into the street. But it was empty.

"Greg?"

"No." A man stepped from the darkness behind her.

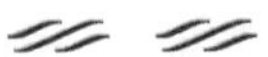

"Greg!" Jia shrieked, racing down the street. She'd been a track star in college, but those days were way behind her now. She filled her lungs with air and her chest burned. She pumped her arms to gain speed, but it wasn't fast enough.

There weren't enough steroids in Lance Armstrong's house to get her legs working right. They were gelled with fear.

"Come back, girl," the man called out as he walked in her direction. Greg was nowhere in sight. He'd disappeared or driven off and Jia had to fight this guy on her own.

What could she do? Running wouldn't work, he kept pace easily, and if she hid… she scanned the shadows of the buildings, short beneath the light of the moon and swallowed. There was nowhere to hide.

Nowhere to run, nowhere to hide. This was a horror movie in real life.

She stopped and turned, channelling a few weeks' worth of

anger into her facial muscles. "Who are you?"

He pushed a pair of circular glasses up his chubby caramel-colored nose. "I'm Jia Kailai."

She reeled, then braced herself against the hood of a car. The bonnet was cold and the window had been hit by a brick: the circular puncture had sent spidery cracks through the glass in concentric circles.

"The fake profile." Jia forced her lips together.

"Smart girl." He remarked, moving forward a few feet. His walk was important, he didn't so much step as swagger toward her, and it didn't match his soft body, or the amiable expression he wore for armor.

Every nerve ending in her body screamed for her to run. But there was nowhere to go. He blocked her path back to the Anonymous safe house.

"Who are you really?" But she had the information already: she'd traced the hacker on the internet, the man who'd put up her profile and had targeted him on one of the hacker chats she frequented.

She'd been so consumed with the Facebook project, she'd left his background check on the back burner.

He still hadn't answered her, but reached into his pocket.

"Hold it right there," she yelled, and he let out a low laugh which travelled between them and reverberated off the plain concrete buildings. Cats meowed and knocked over a cluster of trash cans nearby.

"I'm the man who's going to set the world right."

"Stay back or I'll –"

"You'll what?" He laughed again, his sneakers – who the hell wore sneakers with a suit? – made a strange puff each time he shifted them.

"Greg!" Jia tried one last time, screaming it over her shoulder.

"Bad move," the hacker, Anand Vermugante, said.

"Jia?" Davoli's voice drifted back to her and hope leapt up and pounded along with her pulse.

"Greg, I'm here," she shrieked it and spun around, searching between cars and buildings for him. The shadows and alleys blurred into a line, and she panted, praying for him to appear.

Heavy footfalls rushed up behind her, and the cool circle of the end of Anand's gun pressed against her temple. "Keep quiet."

Anand's stubby hand fondled her, groping through her clothes and settling on the necklace she wore. She'd strung the flash drive containing the Paradigm data around her neck.

"Got you," Anand whispered in her ear. His breath smelled of curry fish tacos and she gagged on the stench.

"Let go of me," she hissed back, but he didn't loosen his grip on the drive or on the gun. He shifted her backward, dragging her by the chain.

Where was Greg? She scanned for him constantly – if only he'd rush around the corner and tackle Anand. Use that damn FBI training for something other than judging her every move.

Anand stopped beside a navy blue Mercedes-Benz with

blacked-out windows. He wrenched the door open and it made a violent clunk. He forced her into it. Pulling on that chain so hard it cut into the flesh around her throat.

He took the gun off her for a second.

"Greg!" Jia screamed, but the car door slammed in her face and she was doused in the scent of expensive leather seats and a whiff of the accusing tacos from a take out box in the back.

She glared out the window and tried the handle.

"They're locked, sweetheart." Anand appeared in the driver's seat and grinned at her with two rows of perfectly white teeth. "I'll take that," he said and gripped the flash drive. He gave a quick yank and the chain snapped off her neck.

"What do you want with me?"

"I want the world and you're going to help me get it." He started the car and Greg appeared behind them, sprinting, arms pumping hard. "Looks like your friend is late. Sorry about that."

Jia didn't want to lose him, but Anand put his foot down and they sped off, down the road. He took a sharp right, then left, and continued the turns until Jia was disoriented.

"I can't help you get anything. You have the flash drive, you have what you want, so just let me go."

"I don't have what I want yet, but your skills are going to help me get it."

Jia gripped the loose seatbelt and searched for any object she could use as a weapon.

"Move and you're dead. I've got the back seat rigged with a

high-pressure explosive. It's localized, so it'll take you out with minimal damage to me. Do anything I don't like, and you're gone. Understand me?"

He could've been lying, but she didn't know enough about explosives to take her chances.

"You're crazy." Who was this guy really? Jia swallowed hard and gripped the seat with both hands. Please let her not have been right about the Gang of 8, about the hacker. "What do you want?"

"All in good time, Ms. Kailai. Perhaps, if you do as I ask, I will provide you with the information you're after."

"You're a terrorist, aren't you?" She couldn't keep the remark down any longer.

"That's astute of you. I suppose to your 'civilized' mind, I would be a terrorist. Really, I am a harbinger of the true way. I bring news about your future: it doesn't end well for you." Anand's hands were calm on the steering wheel.

Whatever passion he had for his cause was hidden. He wasn't the kind of psycho terrorist she'd seen on the news. Those bushy-haired dudes with the long beards and the wild look in their eyes.

He was different. He had this calm veneer, a coating over that ruthless nature or greed for power.

Jia shivered and gripped her arms, then fastened her seatbelt. Anand gave a nod and focused those beady eyes on the road. Buildings zipped past, brick facades mocking in the half-light. She was trapped and she could do nothing but what this guy said.

Or she could escape.

There'd be no bombs outside of the car. She could make a run for it. Head back to Anonymous and gather forces to take him down. Greg would be there – this was a cause he'd definitely rally behind.

The thoughts injected strength into her spine and she wriggled her nose. What was the deal here? Knowledge was power, and the more she had on the puffy Anand Vermugante, the better.

"What's the group? ISIL? ISIS? Al-Qaeda?"

Anand directed the car into a back alley and Jia's throat closed up tight.

"It is called the Islamic State." He answered, and the engine cut out. He jangled the keys out of the ignition and put them in his pocket beside the flash drive.

"Where are we?" She peered out into the darkness. She'd been helpless before, her future plucked from her grasp, but now it was worse. Now, she might not have a darn future at all.

Anand opened the door and got out without answering, then slammed it and came round to her side.

He unlocked for her and she glared up into his eyes, black with shadow and evil.

Anand gestured for her to get out and follow him.

"It's the end of the line."

Greg Davoli raced after the Mercedes.

Jia was in the back and that guy, the one from the Gang of 8, was behind the steering wheel. He'd recognizes him instantly from the case files on the organization.

Anand Vermugante. He was a computer scientist turned criminal, and he'd worked closely with Aceves while Greg had been at Paradigm. The car careened around a corner and sped out of sight.

Greg pumped his arms – he couldn't let her go – and turned onto the next street, but the Mercedes was nowhere in sight.

Disappointment dropped into the pit of his stomach, a lead weight buckling his legs. He leaned against the brick-faced building nearby and tilted his head back to stare at the stars.

Jia had been abducted and he'd been dumb enough to let that happen.

He should've fought for her! He should've tried to see things from her point of view.

"Davoli," a voice called out to him, and he spun, reaching into the waistband of his jeans for the gun which wasn't there.

It was Debra. She marched up the street with her arms folded against the cold, and glanced either way.

"What happened?" She halted in front of him and glared. She'd never liked or trusted him, that much was plain.

"They took Jia."

"What? Who?" Debra pressed a palm over her heart and massaged the spot.

"The Gang of 8. It was Anand Vermugante. I had notes on

him when I was still working with the, uh," he paused and cleared his throat.

"I see." Debra pursed her lips, then relaxed them in increments. "Jia was too confrontational with Twitter. She went after Anand, he took notice, and now it might be too late to get her back and repair the damage done."

"Too late? Too confrontational with Twitter? Debra, you've been the main driving force behind the social media take down. You had Jia convinced it was the right thing to do, when really, it's thinly veiled terrorism. You're just as bad as the Gang of 8. In fact, you're worse. You'd leave Jia to fend for herself, rather than helping her?"

"That's not what I'm saying." Debra's answer was calm, though her eyes flashed with anger which buried itself deep and resided there. "But Anonymous has other priorities, and unless Jia has something which could compromise the group, they won't go out of their way to get her back."

"How honorable. Typical anarchists. You want to break everything down, and when you've done that, you're not interested in putting the pieces back together again." Greg stopped and drew a breath, then shoved himself off the wall. "I need help getting her back."

Debra tapped her mouth with one finger. "I've got a daughter to look after and a dead husband to avenge. I can't physically do anything, Davoli, except lend you the resources to track her down." She shook her head and brushed hair back from her face.

"And even then, I'll have to convince the others to let you back in."

Greg paced back and forth, loafers slapping the pavement. "Why the hell wouldn't I be allowed back in?"

"Jia's missing after your arrival? You're a Fed? You don't really belong near us and if the big guys at the head of the org found out I'd allowed you in, I'd be out on the streets too. I've got to speak to the others. I'm not sure you're worth the risk."

"And you wouldn't do that? For Jia."

"I'll do what I can, Greg," she answered, then sighed and puffed her cheeks out. "But I can't make any promises. I suggest you get yourself a backup plan." She marched off down the road, back to the house they used for a base.

FBI Intel had told him there were several of the beaten houses across the world. Miniature bases of operation which allowed members to come and go, use the facilities, continue with their lives. Granted, a lot of Anonymous members worked from the privacy of their own homes, but the people like Debra, like Jia, they needed safety and the long arm of the rebel group was happy to wrap itself around them and incorporate them.

"Damn it," he cursed. Scrubbing his hands over his cheeks and the five o'clock shadow along his jaw.

What else was there? He couldn't go back to the FBI without risking serious repercussions, and if he did, he'd be tasked with bringing Jia in for questioning. Now, she was involved in Anonymous. Using them to find her meant imprisoning Jia.

But wasn't imprisonment better than death at the hands of the Gang of 8?

Greg sat down on the sidewalk with his feet in the gutter. It was late, but the first streaks of dawn painted the sky a dull gray to match his inner monologue.

"What do I do?" He whispered to himself. He couldn't condemn Jia to death. But he wouldn't let her rot in jail because of her association with Anonymous and now, with the Gang of 8.

His boss wouldn't see it as a coincidence. If Jia was caught, it was over – for her and their relationship.

Greg couldn't go back to the grind, to existing for the job and nothing else. But he'd do it if it meant saving her.

He let out a low groan and gripped his hair. He tugged lightly and let go a moment later.

His phone rang in his pocket and he whipped it out, hope erupting in his chest. But it wasn't Jia.

Greg pressed the green button. "Davoli speaking."

"Davoli, where the hell are you?"

He'd absconded without a word to his superiors. They likely still thought he worked for them and hadn't reported in for a reason other than him not wanting to work for them.

"Carlos, this isn't a good time."

"We've got operatives out looking for you, Greg, where the hell have you been?" Carlos grunted it out.

"I'm sorry, Carlos, but I don't think I can do this anymore." He massaged his temples. This might not be the right thing to do, but he couldn't condemn Jia to a life in prison.

There had to be another way around this. Maybe if he spoke to Debra again, if he begged Anonymous …

"Davoli, I'm going to advise you to clarify your meaning on this." Carlos' voice changed, it sharpened into an arrow and Greg was the target.

"You can record the conversation if you want, but it won't change my answer. I don't work for you anymore."

"Then I'll have no choice but to assume you've gone rogue and have other agents track you down."

They'd track him all right. "I'll see you around, Carlos."

"You can count on that."

The line went dead, but it didn't matter. He needed to get back to Anonymous and get in, so he could do what was right for Jia. If he could find her, he could take Anand down before he caused problems.

Greg rose and dusted himself off, then froze in his tracks. Jia had the flash drive. Anand would be able to use it to get to Cial-Corp, and if he did that, he'd have the top secret information on the IPO. Plus the algorithm.

Greg dashed down the road and to the building, with its unassuming dark wood door. He knocked hard and rattled the knob, but it was shut tight. Footsteps rang out on the other side, locks were drawn back, and the door creaked open.

"Greg, I'll contact you once I have word on whether we can

let you in or not. Now isn't a good time." Debra said it in a hushed whisper, then slipped out into the night again.

"I blew the FBI off, but it doesn't matter. I have to get in and save Jia. I've got a feeling that everyone's fate rests on it." He glanced past her into the darkness of the hall. There were men in there, listening, watching.

Waiting for Debra to call them out?

She wiggled her head in indecision. "It would be better if you left." One of the guys in the passage moved forward, ever so slowly, like he'd corner a wild animal.

"Come on. You've got to help me. You've got to help Jia."

Debra stared him dead in the eye and opened her mouth to answer.

BANG! A bullet whistled past Greg's ear.

Debra fell to the ground with a thump.

CHAPTER 19

It was 7:00 a.m. on a Monday and the sky was a gray with clouds, spitting drizzle onto the sidewalk outside, creating a pattern of wet and dry which was comforting in its familiarity.

Or it should've been.

Mary sat on the edge of her bed in the California motel and stared at the piece of paper in one hand. The worn beige phone – which had once been white – lay beside her, taunting her.

She'd spent thc past week contacting the friends and relatives of Hailey Iglesias.

They said she'd been mentally ill, but Hailey's mother had revealed the truth between hysterical bouts of crying.

Hailey had fallen victim to a vicious attack.

Mary was responsible for some of the soul-destroying grind.

She smoothed the piece of paper with her gnarled thumb and gulped. She had to be at work in an hour. Better to get it over and done with now, then she could move on.

Though, there wasn't much of a life left for her.

Greg Davoli was last on her list of relatives. He was Hailey's uncle and hopefully, speaking to him would provide a form of closure on what had happened.

Her fingers shook, but she picked up the receiver, pegged it between her shoulder and ear, and dialed the number. It rang three times.

"Davoli speaking," he said, and her mouth went dry.

"Hello, Mr. Davoli. My name is Mary Dorowski and I need to talk to you about your niece, Hailey."

Greg went silent and she toyed with a hole in the faded bedspread.

"I understand this call is unexpected, but I've spoken to your sister and her family, and I felt I should speak to you next."

"What's this got to do with the Gang of 8?" He barked it out and her eyelids fluttered in an involuntary twitch.

"I – It has nothing to do with them." Mary pressed three fingers over her eye and breathed to steady her nerves. "How do you know about that?"

"Mrs. Dorowski, I worked with the FBI on the case to take down that criminal syndicate."

"Oh good God, there's no escaping you people. I didn't call to talk about my husband or Taylor or anyone else but your niece. Is that clear, young man?" Her attempt at motherly discipline was feeble. She'd lost touch with reality after weeks in the motel room, days spent bagging groceries.

"I suggest you get to the point quickly."

She gulped over and over again. There was dead silence and she didn't want to break it to admit to what had happened. What she'd done to destroy the lives of people she barely knew, but who deserved life, love and happiness as much as the next God-fearing person.

"I'm calling because of Hailey and what happened to her."

"All right," he said, drawing it out in suspicion. There was the tap of keys in the background, which dropped off immediately at the mention of the girl's name.

"Mr. Davoli, I feel responsible for your niece's attempted suicide and I needed to tell you what happened so that you could get some closure on the incident. Of course, that would provide me with closure, too." Mary broke off, took a breath, and continued, "I want you to know that I didn't realize what would happen and how wrong I was to do this until it was too late." Her throat grew thick with emotion and she reached for the glass of water on the bedside table.

"With all due respect, Mrs. Dorowski, what the hell are you talking about?" There was stress in his voice and she itched to slam the receiver down and try again later. She was afraid of how he'd react, not that she could do anything if he was angry or even that he could harm her, but she wanted to know that it was all right.

That on some level she hadn't destroyed a family. That she could be forgiven.

"I stumbled upon the pictures of Hailey on Facebook and I got angry." Mary ripped at the hole in the sheets and it tore open to reveal the stuffing below. "I re-posted the videos and pictures. I didn't think it would make such a huge impact on the media. Or on Hailey's life." Tears welled up and spilled onto her cheeks, but she didn't dab at them. She let them flow and drip onto the keypad of the phone.

"I see." Davoli didn't say more than that. He left the sentence hanging between them and she forced her mouth open again.

"It wasn't vindictive, I just –"

"That's exactly what it was. I don't know what's going on in your life, but there's no excuse to spread lewd pictures of another person. There is no excuse. Do you understand that?"

"I understand, but I was trying to –"

"Trying to what? Make the world aware of a young girl's troubles? Even if she'd participated in those acts willingly, it wasn't your place to spread or comment on that. It wasn't your place to judge or ridicule her."

Mary huffed a few times. Even Hailey's mother had been more understanding than this.

"I was angry, I didn't think about it, I just clicked through and sent the pictures."

"That's the problem with the world, Mrs. Dorowski. It's too easy to hurt someone else without thinking, especially if it makes you feel better."

"It wasn't like that!" Mary cried, shaking her head frantically, though he couldn't see her. She glanced at the clock – she had to be at work in 15 minutes.

"It was exactly like that. I don't have time for people like you, Mary. I hope one day you realize that the world isn't your sandbox and people aren't your toys. You're a despicable example of humanity, you deserve prison as much as the next rapist or killer, because of what you did." he said, then broke off and took a breath fraught with pressure before continuing. "What you did is just as bad as murder. I will never forgive you for this."

Click. The dial tone left a low buzz of anxiety and sorrow in her ear.

She hadn't meant to hurt anyone. She'd lost a lot, she'd been so angry that others had freedom and happiness, while she was stuck in some tiny motel working after years of comfort.

Mary stumbled up, tears flowing, and made for the door. She had to get to work before she lost that job too. She snatched up her purse on the way out.

She wore her best pair of slacks and a clean white cardigan over a white camisole. She walked the four blocks to work.

The morning air was crisp with a slight chill and Mary tugged her cardigan close and put her head down as she walked. At this time, if she were at home, the sun would have just risen over the roof of the Williams' house. The sunlight would stream in through the stained glass of her front door, creating a Technicolor display on the wood floors of the foyer.

Once, long ago, the kids had played in the colored spots on the floor. The tears kept on, trailing down and wetting her cardigan.

The hum of an engine interrupted her melancholy traipse and she frowned and glanced back. There was a car driving slowly behind her. She put some pep in her step.

There were few people about in this area at this time. No one would notice if she was robbed or grabbed off the street by hooligans. She hugged her purse and walked as fast as she could.

She heard a familiar chuckle. Then, a male asked, "Where are you going in such a hurry?"

"I'm sure that stalking is illegal; even for law enforcement Mr. Perez," Mary replied.

Perez laughed again and continued on down the street. The vehicle reached the junction and took the left turn leading back into town.

Panic built inside her chest – she was under surveillance that much was clear. She was a germ under their microscope, exposed to them and primed for whatever experiment they had in mind.

Her teeth chattered, but at least the tears were gone, for now. She pushed open the convenience store door and walked up to the Asian man who'd hired her. She wouldn't try pronouncing his name. It was gibberish to her anyway.

"Good morning! You nice and early Mrs. Drowsky," he greeted her with the enthusiasm she didn't share; especially because he pronounced her name wrong. "Put down bag in here in locker. It will be safe. I promise. Put down bag." He motioned for her to place her bag on a wooden shelf behind the cash register. She complied reluctantly.

Then he smiled at her, rattled off something and beckoned for her to follow him into the back.

Thank goodness for hand signals.

They entered the door leading into the storage room, and her employer spun around and darted behind the maze of shelves. Mary gasped. There were three agents with their guns out, directed at her forehead. Sergeant Perez and his partner came up behind them with smug looks on their faces.

"Mrs. Dorowski, you are under arrest."

CHAPTER 20

"Where are you, Tay?" Debra whispered. There was no one else in the room with her and it was late. She hunched over the computer, sifting through documents about Midnight Havoc.

The government hadn't returned his remains and Shannon was insistent that he was alive. She reminded Debra each morning and night that Daddy would be home soon.

But there was nothing, no evidence that Taylor was alive or that he'd been in Midnight Havoc for that matter, apart from the fact that he was stationed at the base in Syria.

"Debra!" A man spoke beside her and she jumped. The usual hope sprang up and then melted into nothingness again. It would never be Taylor beside her again.

"I'm sorry to interrupt, but I need to use one of these PCs. Do you mind?"

"Do what you want, Greg." She didn't raise her gaze to meet his. Just because they'd allowed him in, didn't mean she had to like him. He'd led Jia astray from the start, and the shooting incident the day before and the fact she had to throw herself on the ground was proof: Greg Davoli was nothing but trouble.

"I need your help." He didn't move away to the other work station.

"With what? I'm kind of busy with something personal right now." She minimized the search she'd opened and turned to him at last.

"Finding Jia and Anand."

"You're more qualified than I am to do that, Davoli." Debra sighed and blinked her exhaustion away. She got up and walked to the coffee pot on the counter nearby, then poured herself a cup.

"I need as much help as I can get on this. The less time it takes, the more chance I have of saving her before we lose everything."

"We?"

"Jia had sensitive data with her. The kind that could bring on a whole mess of trouble if it falls into the wrong hands."

"Greg, I want to help Jia but I've got to stay focused. I've got a lot at stake." Debra squished the Styrofoam cup, threw it in the trash can at the end of the table and reached for another.

"Yeah, you're not the only one. If we don't get Jia back, you won't have the opportunity to find Taylor."

She slammed the coffee pot down and it cracked. "Don't talk about him."

"Debra, I just got off the phone with a woman who mentioned him. She was intimately involved with the Gang of 8, or at least her husband was. That's too much of a coincidence to ignore."

"What are you saying?"

Greg motioned for her to sit, but she stood strong, gripping the Styrofoam cup and glaring him dead in the eye.

"Jia had this theory, and I ignored it until now, but she believed that the Gang of 8 was involved in terrorist activities somehow."

"And you're saying my husband was a terrorist." She breathed through her nose.

"No, that's not what I'm saying. But you need to know the truth about Midnight Havoc and Anand Vermugante."

Debra wrinkled her forehead then massaged it. "Enlighten me."

"Anand had access to Jia's Facebook profile. In all honesty, he was the one who created it in the first place."

"Yeah, Jia mentioned something about that. She's been obsessed with finding the guy who did it since then, but what's this got to do with Taylor?" Debra sipped the coffee and savoured it, calming herself with the aroma and the taste.

"Debra, you posted pictures to Jia's wall. Christmas pictures of Taylor in Syria at the base. These pictures had embedded geotarget information. I'm afraid Anand used the GPS data embedded on those pictures to locate the base and aid the attack."

"That's impossible." She denied it with every piece of her core. There wasn't a chance she'd been the one who'd gotten Tay in trouble, who'd jeopardized the base.

"The other explanation is that Taylor or one of the others was a traitor, but given that Anand is working so hard to get his hands on Jia and the information on CialCorp…"

"I don't understand."

"It's simple. If Anand is at fault, Taylor is innocent. If he is, Midnight Havoc might be partly your fault." Greg didn't pull any punches, but that was the way she preferred it.

"I still don't understand why Anand wants Jia."

"Because Jia has information which Anand could use to destroy everything this country stands for."

Debra snorted and drank the coffee to hide the pain which sat between her eyes. She was the one who'd started this, who'd hurt Taylor and everyone else in his unit. She was to blame.

"In case you've forgotten, I'm against what this country stands for. They believe my husband was a terrorist, they've effectively taken away my daughter's future because of that."

"The only one who has any say over your daughter's future is you," Greg retorted. "And if we don't stop Anand from getting that data, she might not have one at all. Do you understand me?" He moved in close and she recoiled, putting up that glare of disdain. Inside, she'd broken apart again.

She had to make this right somehow.

"Fine." Debra whispered it in a long stream of anger. "But not one word of this to the others."

"As if I'd involve anyone else." Davoli sauntered past her and took a seat at a computer nearby. "I need you working on their location. No doubt he'll not realize we can trace Jia's phone via location services or surveillance cameras. Let's find an electronic trail and find Jia." He leaned over the keyboard and tapped away, bringing up pages and searching names before she'd moved an inch.

"I know what to do, Davoli, I just don't like doing it." Debra didn't want to admit that she'd jeopardized her family out loud. She was too hard for that now, she'd gone too far since she'd been a housewife in Coppell, baking cookies and praying for Taylor to come home.

If she could be part of something bigger this time around, maybe that was a good thing. Taylor would've died for the United States. She'd do this for him, to atone for the mistakes she'd made and the reliance she'd had on Facebook and Twitter and every other social media platform.

"Debra, are you ready to do this?" Greg leaned back and the chair squeaked beneath him.

"Yes," she answered and went to her station. She stretched, yawned and arranged herself in her chair. This was for Taylor.

CHAPTER 21

The lights were way too bright. Her head pounded and she gripped it, leaning her elbows on the steel table in the interrogation room.

Mary's life was over, but it seemed it was no less than she deserved after what had happened to Hailey. The tears were back and she let them flow unfettered.

The questions were foreign to her and she didn't have any answers. There was something about an IP address and illegal activity. Investment scams and the Gang of 8.

That one kept cropping up. Gang of 8 and Len. Her dearest Len, who'd been a criminal according to them.

"I had nothing to do with any of it. I don't know about any of it." She repeated the mantras for the 20 millionth time.

"That's interesting, Mrs. Dorowski, but we have information which states otherwise," Perez said, tapping his knuckles on the table. "Otherwise you wouldn't be here. Now, do us all a favor, save yourself some time and tell me what you know."

Mary gathered that the interest in the heads of the gang was on a Federal level, but she still didn't understand why they thought that a retired old woman, who could barely figure out how to call her family on Skype, could be orchestrating such activities with enough finesse to evade authorities.

"Let's try this again Mrs. Dorowski. Your husband was one of the founding members of the Gang of 8. Who were his closest associates at the time?"

"I don't really know. He kept a lot to himself and he died 15 years ago."

"Listen, stop playing games with us." Perez leaned forward and snatched up a glass of water. He gulped it down and cleared his throat. "We've already found out that major transactions involved in the investment scam were running through your IP address. There's evidence of hacking, clickjacking and spam. Your IP address is a hotspot of activity, Mrs. Dorowski, and you'd like us to believe that you have had nothing to do with it just because you present yourself as an innocent old lady?"

Mary breathed through her open mouth, but there wasn't enough oxygen in the world to calm her down.

She'd made so many mistakes. She'd caused the demise of an innocent girl. She'd lost everything because of her trusted husband. She was innocent of one crime and guilty of another in her eyes.

It seemed like no matter what answer she gave or how much she explained that she had no idea what they were talking about, they were adamant she was guilty.

The quiet partner finally spoke up. "We know you're not working alone and we doubt that the big guys are too chummy cause y'know … you've got to keep things stealthy to keep the Feds off your trail right? Tell us. Who is your contact?"

His voice was ice cold and only his mouth moved when he spoke. There wasn't any emotion in him, because he didn't care about Mary.

She was a pawn to be used. He wanted names, he wanted to know more about the Gang of 8 and he wouldn't stop until she gave him what he wanted. But she didn't know anything.

Mary didn't say a word. Nor did she call for a lawyer. She'd been told that innocent people didn't need one.

"The silent treatment, huh? Well, let me ask you something, would you start talking if we asked you about your nephew, Taylor?"

She couldn't hide her reaction to his name.

"Ahh! That struck a nerve didn't it?" He sat back in the chair. It squeaked with the effort of supporting his shift in weight. The ever-quiet Agent Maloney stood facing her with his back to the wall of two-sided glass. His gaze never left her face. He narrowed his eyes and gritted his teeth.

Agent Perez pressed on, "Mrs. Dorowski, can you explain how you managed to get into contact with a man who is assumed dead and considered responsible for the attack."

"Taylor wouldn't hurt a fly." She insisted, jabbing the table with her forefinger to provide some kind of strength to her argument. She didn't have enough of it, these days. Kids, grandkids, cooking, cleaning, that she could do. Pleading innocence convincingly was beyond her skillset.

"So you admit you've been in contact with him." Perez gave a small smile and folded his arms.

She couldn't let them hurt Taylor, there wasn't a chance he'd ever betray his country. He had a family waiting at home, poor Debra and Shannon. Taylor would never have sold them out.

"I have nothing to say, but that my nephew wouldn't harm anyone intentionally. He's a good boy."

Maloney glanced at Perez and placed a finger on the groove in his chin. "That's present tense talk, Mary."

"Pardon?"

"You said 'he is a good boy,' not 'he was a good boy'."

"This is ridiculous, you're twisting my words to trick me and I won't have any more of it." Mary's voice cracked. She was moments from cracking apart, but she had to stay strong.

Her eyes were dry from the air conditioning, but they welled up anyway. What had she done to deserve this?

At that moment two guys in black suits burst into the room. One was a middle-aged black male and the other was a Caucasian with a balding crown, who could've been about the same age.

"What are you doing here, Owens?" Perez rose, pushing his chair back and scraping its legs along the floor. "This is our case."

"Relax, kiddo, I'm not here to get involved in the Gang of 8. That storm in a teacup is all yours, sweetheart." The balding guy chuckled.

"What do you want?" Maloney spoke shortly after.

"We're taking over this interrogation, effective immediately." The black agent said, then strode over to the desk and slid into the chair opposite Mary. "Give them the file, Owens." He waved toward his partner.

The agent handed them a brown file, which Maloney and Perez hunched over. They shot each other furtive looks which became angry.

"Cute," Maloney remarked, then shoved the file back at the agent. "We'll be seeing you again soon, Mrs. Dorowski."

Mary didn't answer, but a deep pang of foreboding fired off in her gut. What was this about?

The black agent came over to the edge of the table and slung his one leg over it to take a seat.

Both of them sat staring at her for a lot longer than was deemed polite.

Surprisingly, the man sitting on the edge of the desk was the first to speak. "Mrs. Dorowski, my name is Special Agent Danny Medina with the FBI and with me is NSA agent Travis Owens. What the agents touched on is a matter of National Security. I'm sure by now you have heard of the tragedy in the Middle East being referred to in the media as 'Midnight Havoc.' Am I right?"

"I'm not sure. I think I may have seen it somewhere." It was a lie. Although she honestly had not had any time to pay attention to the story with everything that had been going on with her case. It was nearly impossible for someone to not have heard about it the way that story had been bleated and revisited by every news station in the country.

Agent Medina raised his eyebrow. “Right.”

Owens gave a soft cough – the bravado he’d presented in front of the other agents was gone, replaced by a blank stare. That had to be what they taught these people in agent school.

“Anyway, your nephew Taylor Wins had been deployed on humanitarian efforts in Syria at the time of the attack. He was one of the American soldiers declared dead even though his body could not be found.” Agent Medina narrowed his chocolate-brown eyes, and studied her reactions carefully. “Since his death, there has been an on-going investigation to determine those responsible for the attack and we found evidence that Taylor may have been selling inside secrets on the black market ...”

The agent’s voice faded into background noise.

Mary was light-headed. Her heart beat against her ribs like a caged beast and her stomach squeezed all of its contents up into her throat. She coughed and choked.

She wasn’t sure whether to cry or scream. Taylor had been a son to her. She’d raised him from the age of 7 when his mother appeared on her doorstep in the middle of a rainstorm claiming she needed a few days to visit her sick mother and never came back.

Mary had watched him grow up with his cousins, part of the family, and now he was gone. The room spun to a blur, though she was still seated. A cold chill washed over her as a myriad of distorted voices called her name.

It was too much.

"Mrs. Dorowski?" The agent's words swam through the haze. "Mrs. Dorowski?"

"Yes," she croaked, and glanced up into his face.

"Taylor Wins' name has been cleared. It was discovered that he was sent as a messenger rather than an insider."

Mary gripped the desk with both hands, knuckles turning white. "He's fine? Taylor's fine?"

"Yes, Mrs. Dorowski, but your involvement with the Gang of 8 is suspect. We've been handed information which indicates one of their members may be sponsoring terrorism."

It was a deluge of information and she drowned in it, searching for any sensible piece of knowledge to cling to.

"What's that mean? What's it got to do with me?"

"Well, Mrs. Dorowski, we have reason to believe that you were involved in the funding of the operation that delivered us the Midnight Havoc event, based on your activities related to the Gang of 8."

"Terrorism," she remarked, then caught a glimpse of herself in the window. Curled greying hair, wrinkled skin, terrified eyes. They thought she financed terrorism.

Mary Dorowski melted into a pool of sadness.

The balding agent stood and studied her. "Enough for today. Take this one back to her cell."

They dragged her from the chair, because she was too weak, too finished, to walk.

It was over.

CHAPTER 22

His heart pounded out a drum beat in his chest. This was it.

Jia was inside the building, all the evidence he and Debra had gathered pointed to this exact location.

The sky was peppered with stars, blocked intermittently by dark clouds. They scudded aimlessly, hiding the light for seconds or minutes at a time. One of the windows in the gray apartment block was brightly lit.

A shadow moved across it for a moment, a portly man from what Greg could make out.

It was Anand.

Greg Davoli rolled his shoulders and breathed through his nose. He made a hissing noise in his throat with each exhalation, a trick he'd learned to calm himself. He didn't like this.

There were too many variables to account for here. He didn't have back up. He was on his own and Jia's guts, brain and body were on the line if he messed up.

"It's time," he muttered to himself, drumming his palms on the steering wheel. "It's time." He slipped out of the driver's seat and closed the door. He left the keys in the ignition in case they needed to make a quick getaway. He glanced both ways, but the street was clear, apart from a few cats near an overflowing trash can.

Anand likely planned on removing Jia from the country, or killing her. So why hadn't he?

Greg mulled the question over and snuck toward the alleyway. His intelligence told him that there was a side entrance to the building. He'd been unable to access detailed schematics on such short notice, so the knowledge he had of the basic layout would have to do.

He strolled into the alleyway and tried the side door. It was locked. He got down on one knee and brought out his lock-picking kit, inserted it into the keyhole and jiggled until he heard the telling clicks.

He tried the handle and the door swung inward.

He sniffed the air, an old habit, and entered slowly, searching from side-to-side. The hall inside was musty and dimly lit. A single swinging light bulb illuminated the cracked concrete of the walls.

Someone coughed downstairs, but he didn't bother exploring. If Anand was upstairs, it was likely that Jia was with him too.

Greg took the rickety staircase, climbing slowly and keeping an ear out. He stopped on the landing in the dark and listened hard.

"You've given me everything I need without even trying," a man spoke.

"You won't get away with this." That was Jia!

"Famous last words," Anand replied, and Greg clenched his fists. It was now or never. He rushed at the door and burst into the room, ready for a fight.

But the room was empty, bare except for a dirty spotted carpet on the floor and a tape recorder on top of it.

"You've given me everything I need without even trying." The conversation came from the tape recorder, playing on repeat.

It was a trap.

Greg turned, but it was too late. A massive shape crashed into him and tackled him to the ground. He fought back, using every ounce of his training, but the man was too strong.

He pressed a knife to Greg's throat.

"Move and I'll slit your throat open, American pig." The sour smell of old booze followed the whistle of the attacker's words. He had a heavy Iranian accent, and a neatly trimmed beard.

"You don't know who you're dealing with," Greg warned and the attacker chuckled a laugh and pressed the knife in closer.

He shuffled to one side and tugged Greg to his feet. He was a huge guy. This wouldn't be easy. He pulled Greg's pistol from the back of his jeans and pocketed it.

"You come with me now. You're going to see Anand." He dragged him toward the door, but Greg gave no resistance. Seeing Anand meant saving Jia, and the longer he led this fool to believe he was weak, the better.

The assailant marched him down the stairs and into a basement, wreathed in the glow of a single gas lamp. There was no electricity in the basement, apparently, or it was used for something else.

Greg eyed the wires hanging from the ceiling, connected to a chair against the wall.

"Nice to have you with us, Mr. Davoli," Anand stepped from the shadows with a smirk. "We've been expecting you for quite some time."

"Sorry to keep you waiting," Greg answered, and the knifed thug gave him a push.

"Leave him, he will do nothing now," Anand said, fingering a gun in one hand. The thug listened and strode off to stand near the door. Jia was a few feet away, unbound and afraid.

She mouthed something at Greg, but he couldn't make it out.

Anand seemed too relaxed. Perhaps the power had gone to his head.

"You see, I've been waiting for you and your federal friends to catch up. It seems I'm always one step ahead, it's quite disappointing really." Anand smiled and scratched his chin with the end of the gun.

Jia mouthed the word again and shifted slightly. Greg watched her from his peripherals, but he still had no clue what she wanted. Apart from freedom of course.

"What do you want, Anand, why are you doing this?" Greg pushed back with the question, and kept his eye on Jia.

"What I want is to do what should have been done many years ago. End the United States, bring it to its knees."

Greg froze and studied the burly attacker, then flicked his gaze to Anand's face. "Al Qaeda?"

"Hah! Of course not, those fools don't have the ability to do what I do. What we do," Anand said, glancing at his helper nearby.

"The Islamic State." Greg Davoli gritted his teeth and nodded. He'd known all along, but better to have Anand think he had Greg off balance. He'd be easier to work with.

Jia mouthed it again, 'Distraction,' and Greg coughed slowly as a signal to tell her she could stop.

"I worked long and hard with those fools, the Gang of 8, to get what I needed, only to have it ruined by that idiot Aceves." Anand clenched his fist around the gun, finger nowhere near the trigger. "But thanks to lovely Jia over here, I have what I've wanted all along."

"And what's that?"

"The exact details of the algorithm, the process, the schematics, the key codes, the stealth module, the compiler, etc."

"Big Data," Jia said, and the thug shoved her back. She hit the wall and slumped against it, breathing hard.

"Yes, the algorithm will provide me with every bit of information on every consumer in America. And in a fraction of a second reliable predictability. With this we can control the markets."

"Great. The Islamic State can set out a great ad campaign," Greg answered. He'd bought some time for Jia to recover, but she still breathed heavily. It had to be an act. She'd wait on his signal.

"Idiot," Anand spat, "with these details, I can destroy you all. I can bring you to your knees, I can – "

Greg didn't wait for the egotistical litany to end.

He leapt at the terrorist, closing the distance in a heartbeat. The world slowed in that time, reality was drawn out in a long thin stream of activity and he was aware of every bead of sweat on the other man's face.

Anand raised the gun.

Jia bounded upward and knocked the knife from the thug's hand.

Greg's knuckles connected with Anand's jaw.

The thug dived for Jia.

Anand crumpled like a paper doll, but the thug wouldn't give in that easy.

Greg spun on the spot, shaking his right hand and denying the pain. Jia was on the floor, grappling with the cement to get at the knife. Anand's massive colleague took exception to this.

He rammed the heel of his boot onto the back of Jia's neck and she collapsed with a shriek of pain, reaching backward to grip at the monstrous foot.

"Oh no you don't," Greg muttered, then dived at the assailant. He hooked upward with his right fist and connected with his bearded jaw, but the guy didn't collapse as Anand had.

Instead, he turned. "Soft American fool."

"I suppose you pull the legs off goats up in Iran, do you, terrorist?" Greg spat, but the behemoth of a man didn't have time for chit-chat. He came at Greg, who tried to fight back.

The blow landed in the flesh of Greg's stomach and he doubled over at the pain.

"Greg," Jia croaked, but he couldn't respond. A thick ropy arm reached down and gripped him around the neck. The stink of sweat filled his nostrils, and he hit back with his elbows. He hit rock-hard muscle.

Gray speckles clouded his vision. There was Jia on the floor, reaching for something.

"Watch out," she cried, "watch out!"

Heat spread up his neck and he struggled to swallow. Greg turned his head in slow motion. Anand was up and his gun pointed directly at Greg. His finger was on the trigger.

The room had blurred, time had slowed to the beat of his heart, pumping flashes of energy and death. He had no fight left, but he had to fight. For Jia.

Anand squeezed the trigger. Jia sprang from the ground with the knife in hand and tackled him back.

The flare of the gun consumed Greg and a searing pain sprang up in his left shoulder. The thug's arms fell away from his neck and he gasped for air, then stumbled forward a few paces.

Jia was on top of Anand, but neither of them moved.

Greg coughed and gripped his throat, but kept going. She couldn't be dead, he wouldn't allow it. The speckles in his vision retreated, inch-by-inch. There was a low rush of sound which was magnified a second later.

Cognisance was back.

"Jia," he gasped, and stumbled forward to the mess of arms and legs. He didn't search for the attacker. He had to get her out of there, alive, before anything else happened.

She had to be alive. She had to be.

Greg grabbed her by the shoulders and rolled her from Anand's chest. There was blood down her front and her eyes were closed.

"Jia," he said, gathering her in his arms, and stroking her cheek, "Jia, come on, you can't do this to me."

He thumbed her eyelid back.

"Ow!" She winced and glared up at him. "What the hell are you doing, Fed?" But the protest was weak. There was too much blood on her clothes for her to have survived.

"How is this possible?"

Jia was green around the gills, with her lips pressed together tight. "I guess, I'm quicker than I think." She pointed to Anand and Greg eyed the unconscious terrorist with the big plans.

He lay supine, staring at the ceiling with the gun in one hand and a mobile phone in the other. His chest wasn't moving and the hilt of the terrorist's long knife stuck out of it.

Jia had got him right in the heart.

"Come on, let's get out of here." Greg grabbed his left shoulder and grimaced against the pain.

"You're not going anywhere." The other terrorist rose nearby, clutching his upper left arm. His gaze was filled with revenge. Greg gritted his teeth. There was no way he could take on this guy with a busted arm.

"It's over, your master is dead," Jia yelled, but he didn't respond. He was fixed on Greg, drawn forward, magnetized by the need to fight and be fought. The need to kill, even though he had no real reason, other than the call of some 'higher power.'

"He has no master," Greg answered. "Anand was a pawn, he just didn't realize it. There's still something you want in here, isn't there?" He directed that question at the terrorist.

"What is it?" Jia glanced around, studying the gas lamp, the cracked walls and the concrete floor. "What is it?" She said it more to herself than to either man, Greg could tell from the glaze on her eyes.

Greg fumbled along the floor, scrambling backward until his warm fingers met Anand's cooling ones. It was a horrid sensation, touching a dead thing, but it wasn't his first rodeo.

He swept the gun from the corpse and cocked it.

The terrorist slowed, but didn't stop coming. He wanted it, whatever it was, he wanted it.

"Don't come any closer," Greg warned. But it was already too late. He'd done enough work in the field to identify the look in the terrorist's eyes. It was death solidified.

The man was set on his course, even if it killed him. There were no more words to stall him. It was over, one way or another.

He read the thought and charged at Greg, growling, a man possessed.

"Stop," Jia screamed, but Greg didn't try anything else.

He squeezed the trigger, the gun fired, the mountain of a man dropped to the floor. Greg gave Jia a sidelong glance, but she had her palms pressed to her face.

"It's okay, he's gone now."

"You don't say," Jia snapped and sat up straight. She didn't look at the terrorist's body, but gestured to Anand. "Get the phone."

"What's your idea?" Greg snatched it from the dead guy's grip and shrugged off the creeped out shivers climbing his spine.

"Anand took my flash drive, he got access to all the information he mentioned. And he left yesterday to go run an 'errand.' Left me with that psycho over there for three or four hours."

"Sorry about that," Greg answered, then gave her the cell.

"It's whatever." Jia's upper lip twitched on the right side. "The point is, he left to do something and I have a hunch what that might be." She lifted the smartphone and showed him the screen.

It was lit with lines of code.

"He's got it." Jia sighed through her clenched jaw. "And he's already sent it off to several people via an encrypted file transfer protocol account."

"So, we gain access to the account and use the sent emails to identify the locations of the major players. Problem solved."

"Yeah, it would be if we had the resources for this. But we don't." Jia held the phone out to him.

"No, Jia, no. I don't see how –"

A siren blared above their heads and they both froze and glared at each other.

"Time to go," Greg said, and grabbed her by the upper arm. He hauled her up, then half-collapsed onto her under the pain in his shoulder. Jia held him fast and they limped toward the exit together.

The cops had arrived on the scene, perhaps a neighbor had alerted them to the gunshots. Anand had obviously never planned to use the weapon. He'd thought he was invincible.

They climbed the stairs as fast as their legs could take them, then stopped in front of that back door.

"This is it," Greg whispered.

A man's voice wailed over a loudspeaker around the front.

"Come out with your hands in the air."

CHAPTER 23

It was over.

Debra sat staring at the computer screen. She'd helped take down Twitter, she'd attacked Facebook, she'd gone after every terrorist cell's presence on the internet, but none of it mattered.

No matter how much she searched or hacked, she couldn't bring Taylor back. She couldn't give Shannon her father and she couldn't clear her beloved husband's name.

How had it come to this?

Their lives had been so perfect. He'd served his country, she'd served him, and Shannon had been happy. The little girl who'd once been alive with hope, was silent, withdrawn into her own bubble.

Perhaps it was Debra's fault for not paying enough attention or for being consumed by her need to find Tay.

"Mommy?" Shannon stood in the doorway, wearing her pink frock and holding the doll her father had bought her for Christmas the year before.

Debra glared at the screen for a moment longer.

"Yes, Darling?" She softened her voice as much as she was

capable after the pain of losing Taylor and the frustration of her search.

She'd failed him and her daughter. She'd believed she had to do it on her own, but she'd been right since the start: she simply wasn't equipped to help anyone. Let alone herself.

"Mommy, I want to go now."

"Go where, Love? It's not Saturday." On weekends they'd take a trip into town, disguised as a normal mother and child on an outing to the store. They'd buy supplies for Anonymous, maybe get an ice cream as a treat, then head back to base.

"No Mommy, I want to go away forever. I don't like it here anymore. I think it's time for us to leave."

Shannon was right. She'd had the knack of tapping into the emotions and thoughts of others since she'd been a toddler. Holding Debra's cheeks when she was sad and telling her not to worry, Daddy would be home soon.

"We can't go yet, Shannon."

The girl shook her brown curls, and they didn't bob the same as they had back in Coppell. Nothing was the same anymore. They were on the run from the FBI, the NSA, all because of Taylor's supposed treason.

There had to be a way …

"Debra, where's Solo?" A young woman strolled in. She had a heavy Russian accent and a penchant for flowery perfumes. She was stroppy at best, but Debra wasn't afraid of anyone.

"No idea, Tinka." She opened her arms and Shannon rushed

into them and crawled right into her lap. Debra's heart melted for the girl.

"That's no help. We've got trouble with Facebook. Can't keep that sucker down for very long, it seems."

Tinka pronounced 'very' as 'berry' and 'that' as 'dat.' At Anonymous, it didn't matter which country the member hailed from, or who they were, just that they shared the common goal. Take down the establishment, strike back at injustice.

"There's not much I can do about that right now."

Tinka folded her burly arms and looked Debra up and down. "What's your problem?"

"I don't have a problem," Debra barked, and tensed. Shannon made a soft noise and snuggled closer, burying her face in her mother's blouse. "But you seem set on presenting me with one."

"What does that mean?" Tinka's brows drew down into one large line.

"It means I've got a child in my lap and plenty of work to do. It means you'd better get the hell out of my face before I make you. And it means that if you don't, you'll sorely regret it. You get that, Russian Bear?"

Tinka moved back, jaw dropping open. She wasn't used to receiving open hostility, only supplying it to others. She glared for a couple seconds, but didn't linger longer than that.

She turned on her heavy booted heel and clumped out of the room, leaving the banks of computers in relative silence.

It was the middle of the day, and most of the other members

were out and about or taking cat naps. Many preferred to work at night because of the privacy, but they all ended up working together anyway.

Then as one, they'd migrate to day work and end up stuck with the same problem all over again. It was absurd, but funny.

Debra made a point of opposing the trend.

Shannon shook in her arms, and Debra patted her back, running a finger along her daughter's spine. It was a habit she'd picked up from Taylor – he'd done it to Shannon when she was a baby to calm her.

"What's going to happen, Mommy? I'm scared."

"Don't worry, everything will be fine." Would it be? It might be a lie. No, Debra had to make it all right somehow. There had to be a way to find or help Taylor.

She clicked once on her mouse and opened up the home page on her browser. She kept it on CNN in case any relevant news cropped up.

Taylor's face was on the page, highlighted by the text scrolling beneath it.

Debra's heart stopped. Then gave a flutter of palpitations.

Suspected traitor cleared of all charges.

She'd been the reason Midnight Havoc had happened, or so Jia had insinuated, and she'd blamed herself for Taylor's death ever since. This was a tiny beacon.

"Mommy?"

Debra glanced down at her daughter, a smile growing on her

lips. The first expression of joy she'd allowed herself in many months.

"Mommy, you're crying."

"Yes, Darling, it's because I'm happy. And I think you're right, it is time for us to leave this place." Debra helped her daughter stand – with the NSA and FBI focused on other avenues, they'd be free to live their lives. Even if they had to do it without Taylor.

Suddenly, that didn't seem so scary anymore.

"Really? We can go?"

"Yes," Debra answered, gripping the girl's hand. She led her out of the hellish computer room and down the sparsely lit corridors of the beaten house. They made their way out into the sunshine of the street.

Debra's car was parked nearby, and they increased their speed, Shannon skipping toward it. "We're really going? Really, really?"

"Yes, Shannon, we're going to start a new life now." Debra ruffled her daughter's hair and lifted her arms to the sky, absorbing the sunshine.

"With Daddy?" Shannon's hope created a crack in the happiness.

She took a breath and her arms dropped to her side. She lowered herself to Shannon's eye-level and looked her daughter in the eyes, gripping her shoulders.

It was imperative that she understand this once and for all.

"No, I'm sorry, Sweetheart, Daddy is never –"

"Debra." The voice was a dagger through her chest. Her pulse raced and she spun, hair whipping back with the motion.

There was a figure at the end of the road, walking toward her, wearing a plain white T-shirt and worn jeans.

"Debra," he said, and every cell in her body exploded into ecstasy and fear. It was too much to hope. It couldn't be true.

"It's Daddy," Shannon whispered. "It's Daddy!" She yelled, then took off toward him, racing at full speed. Debra stood, took two slow steps, then sprinted alongside her daughter.

Taylor Wins held his arms open.

They collided with him, hugging and kissing his face. He lifted them both in his arms, swung them once, then embraced them further. Every ounce of agony had been worth it, for this moment.

Debra was finally complete. He was back. Taylor was back, and they could have a real life.

She burst into tears, the sobs wracking her body as Shannon bombarded her father with questions.

"Where were you, Daddy? We were so worried that you wouldn't come home. Everybody thought you were dead. They told me so too, but I knew it wasn't true. I knew it." Shannon shone from within, illuminated with that unique glow.

"Taylor," Debra breathed, kissing his cheek softly. It was wet with tears.

He met her gaze and kissed her back, pressing his lips against hers in a crush of love. The affection she'd craved from him, the hard work she'd put in to free his soul when his body was alive and breathing crashed around her. There was no sweeter moment.

There was nothing but Taylor, Debra and their little girl, squished between them, hearts beating as one.

Taylor broke the kiss and gazed into her eyes. "Sorry I'm late."

CHAPTER 24

"There's no way we're making it out of this one," Jia whispered through the darkness.

They were in the hallway which let out the back. The cops were parked out front, a small fleet of cars with their sirens flashing.

"There really aren't that many," Greg replied, grasping her hand. She squeezed gently but he didn't return the gesture. What if he'd leave now that his job was done?

What if it had all been about getting to Anand, and not so much about how he felt for her? Jia waggled her head from side-to-side to try and dismiss the thought.

"You okay?" He glanced at her sideways and she stopped jiggling around like a weirdo.

"I'm fine," Jia answered then pointed at the cop cars outside. "Why are there so few of them?"

"They've got no idea who Anand is or what really happened here, that much is clear. One of the neighbors probably called in about the gunshots." Davoli scratched his chin with the butt of the pistol.

"What do we do?"

"We get out while we can." He tugged her toward the back door and she resisted.

"They'll catch us, Greg, and we don't even know where we're going yet." Jia wasn't too enamored with the concept of running into a couple of Anand's cronies by chance. They had to be out there, somebody would know to check in and when they did, they'd see the cop cars, assume the worst and the hunt would start all over again.

"Does it matter?" He frowned and took up the easy stance he used often – she figured it meant he was a step away from action but still relaxed. "We have to get out of here, we can't stand here talking all day. Why are you delaying, Jia? This is weird."

She stared at him for a good few seconds. Maybe this kinda stuff was normal to him, but it wasn't to her. There were cops out there and evil guys on the horizon.

"Well?" Greg's brow was creased, the look of confusion or irritation.

"Fine, never mind," she said, tossing her hands up in the air and shrugging him off. "Let's get out of here."

"Exactly," he bit back, then snuck out the back door. "Follow me and keep low."

They tiptoed out the back door and stuck to the wall. The bricks scraped her back, but she didn't care that much. The night air was moist and cold, but it didn't stop rivulets of sweat from working their way down her back.

Greg held out a hand and she bumped into him, then leaned over to check the street.

There was a cop car close by, but facing the other way. An officer was perched on its hood, with one foot up against its grill. He didn't seem too concerned about the activity around the front of the house.

To be honest, he didn't seem that concerned about anything at all.

Greg narrowed his eyes at him and whispered, "There's always that one guy." Obviously he had a problem with slackers.

Jia nudged him in the rib cage with her elbow and they snuck past the back of the car. The cop yawned. "Damn graveyard shift," he murmured, and they continued their path past the back of his cruiser.

He froze and turned his head slightly. Jia's heart leapt into her throat.

"What the hell?" The guy spun on the spot drawing out his gun.

Jia was speechless, glued to the spot. They were screwed now. If the cops got their hands on Anand's phone and delayed what had to be done with that information, the consequences could be disastrous.

"Greg Davoli, FBI," he said beside her. He drew out his old badge – he hadn't given it back after he ditched – and flashed the ID at the cop. "We're investigating a matter of National Security and would appreciate your cooperation."

The cop glanced at the gun in Greg's right hand and the badge in the left. Davoli holstered the weapon and tucked the badge into the front pocket of his jeans.

"What's this about National Security?" The cop lowered his gun as he recognized the government-issued service weapon that Greg was holding.

Greg pulled his shirt straight and stretched to increase his height. "Well, Hoskins, it's strictly classified at this point. But I'd appreciate it if you fetch whoever's in charge of this operation."

Hoskins' jaw dropped and Jia's muscles tensed up.

"I don't gotta do nothing for you. I don't report to you," Hoskins growled.

"You're right," Greg said with a calm smile, "but your superiors do. Shall I give them a call and report your behavior?"

The cop clenched his teeth, then spat in disgust. "Wait right here," he answered, and clumped off around the side of the building.

"Run," Greg whispered, and they dashed into the alleyway, losing themselves in the darkness and putting distance between themselves and the building.

"Coulda taken the car," Jia wheezed between massive gulps of air. Her lungs burned, and sweat trickled down her temples. What a damn night.

Greg ran, nursing his arm and wincing from pain every few minutes. He kept pace with Jia, long legs swallowing up the gravel road.

They stopped and rested against the brick wall of a building a few blocks down.

Jia reached into her pocket and checked that Anand's phone was still there. "What now?"

Sirens rang out in the distance. They'd found the bodies, the chase was on.

"Now, we hide from the Feds for the rest of our lives and figure out a way to bring this plot down before they destroy us and everything around us."

"Just another day at the office," Jia quipped. He'd never come back with her to Anonymous, and it was their only option. They needed a base to get things done. They needed the tools to save what they had to save.

"We'd better keep moving."

"I can't run anymore, not without a direction. Feel like a headless chicken," she breathed it out in a long stream of anxiety.

"We don't have much choice," Greg answered, shifting his weight from leg to leg. The sirens were louder, closer.

"There's no way we can do this on our own, Greg."

"Of course, we can."

"Don't be stubborn," she replied, glancing back down the alley. It was empty, but for a few trash cans and a couple stray cats. "We don't have the resources to take down the Islamic State or deal with this darn algorithm on our own. We can sugar coat this all we like, Davoli, but we're deep in the crap here. Knee deep in it, actually."

"I'm not going to the FBI, Jia." Greg shook his head. "That would be counterintuitive."

"I didn't say the Feds!" Jia hissed at him and his brow furrowed. She resisted the urge to smooth the lines away with kisses. She had to stay strong until she was sure he wanted this like she did.

"Anonymous," he said, and raised his shoulders.

"We need the resources to do the right thing here, and they've got everything we need. Look, I won't let social media and the Gang of 8 and the damn Islamic State destroy the lives of anyone else. I've had enough, okay? It's enough." Jia touched her pocket. "I've got the phone, I'll get the info and I'll sort it out and –"

"Save the world all by yourself?" Greg walked over to her and grabbed her by the upper arms. "Face facts, you need me, Jia. We need each other."

"What do you mean?" Hope and excitement blossomed in her chest.

"I mean exactly that. I'm not going on without you in my life. I almost lost you once because of pride and stupidity, and I won't risk losing you again." He drew her closer, wrapped her in his arms.

"But you hate Anonymous, you hate what they stand for."

"No, I hate that they're terrorising innocents in pursuit of a higher cause, but we've got bigger problems right now. If the Islamic State possesses this software there will be attacks, we're all screwed anyway. It won't matter who has privacy or who doesn't."

"So, you're coming with me? We're doing this? We're going to Anonymous for help." She stated the final sentence and he kissed her forehead.

"Yeah, we'll take it on together. Together."

She tilted her head back and stared into his eyes, wishing herself into another place and time where things would be easier, where they could run away together. A world where she didn't have to act hard all the time.

There'd never be a proposal, a wedding, a honeymoon. They could never have kids. They were both outlaws and this was their fate. To run and save the world, to hide and travel.

They were trapped in freedom together.

There was no place she'd rather be.

"Let's go," she whispered and he grabbed hold of her hand.

"Not so fast," a voice spoke up nearby. A man appeared at the end of the alley. He was a silhouette, she couldn't make out who he was, but the moonlight glinted off an object in his hand.

Greg reached for his gun as the man shuffled forward, carrying an almost empty whisky bottle and swinging it left and right. Sweet relief permeated Jia's pores and she sagged again, tension draining away. It wasn't the law, it was just a drunk homeless guy. Man, the city was on its way into the gutter.

"You got any change?" The bum stopped, swaying in his drunken stupor.

"No," Greg and Jia replied in unison, then took off in the opposite direction. Twenty minutes later they were safe, warm, and cradling coffee cups in front of a PC.

"There's nothing more we can do," Jia sighed, leaning back in the chair in the Anonymous house. "There's literally nothing I can do to stop it. Not on my own."

"That's why I'm here," Greg said, pulling up a chair beside her. "What's the problem?"

Jia rapped her knuckles on the desk and ignored the sour stare from another hacker a few feet over. The guy had thick glasses and was hunched over the keyboard, tapping away like a man possessed.

"I've managed to crack a few of the email inboxes, deleted the files, deleted the email from Anand, but there are some I can't get into."

"Okay," Greg said, fine lines of concern crinkling the skin around his eyes, "You can trace them, can't you?"

"I've tried. I can't get exact locations, some of these IP addresses are masked, others are bouncing on servers all over the world. Some of the emails are registered under fake names. All I can do is capture the data and pass it on, Greg."

"There must be another way," he answered, gripping the arm of the chair. "There has to be."

"We don't have that many options. If they have a copy of the algorithm and they figure out how to use it, we are toast."

"How are you this negative, right now? You were the one who

said we should come here, who said we should do this." Greg gestured wildly to the room of computers. "We've got the resources, there's no reason we can't shut them down."

"We need more than exploits, Davoli, come on."

"Can you keep it down, please?" Glasses spoke up and they both pointed at him with a deadly look. He muttered something and bent over his keyboard again.

"More than what we have?" Greg rolled back in the chair and placed both hands on his knees. "Spit it out, Jia, what is it we need?"

She swallowed several times, glanced left and right, then swallowed again. This wouldn't come out easy and it wouldn't go down well.

"We need help."

"What do you mean, help?"

Jia bit her lip. Even she hated admitting this, especially after they'd had to run for 10 blocks to settle down in the base of activity which Davoli despised. This idea wouldn't make it easier on him.

"What kind of help, Jia?" Greg repeated, but there was an expression of anger etched onto him.

"We need the government."

The Anonymous member coughed and spluttered beside his computer, and cast Jia a gaze of utter disdain. She ignored his glare and sighed heavily.

"I'd be the last one to admit it, okay? My life was ruined by the Gang of 8 and the Feds and this whole insane adventure."

"Precisely," Greg said.

"But," Jia interjected, reaching over to squeeze his arm, "this is bigger than me, it's bigger than you, it's bigger than anything right now."

"What about Anonymous? What about taking down social media and destroying the injustices of society?" Greg's tone was scathing. He'd made it abundantly clear how he felt about the 'futile' mission they'd undertaken.

He hated that Anonymous was involved with cyber-terrorism, but hated society for what it'd done to Hailey.

Jia rolled her chair back and forth, contemplating. There really was no other way to do it. No other method of solving the problem. They were out of their league. Two hackers or a thousand and two hackers against the most feared terrorist group of the century? It wouldn't work.

They weren't superheroes. They weren't even vigilantes.

"Davoli, if we don't stop the Islamic State, there won't be an Anonymous and there certainly won't be a society left to change." Jia saved the info on a MicroSD and slid them into a yellow envelope with the FBI director's name printed in bold type on the front. She'd placed an encryption key which would alert her the minute it was used and the file was opened. She placed Anand's phone in the envelope and sealed it all up.

"I can't condone this."

"We have to go to the FBI and give them everything."

"You go to the FBI and they'll take you along with all your data and knowledge." Greg interjected, fists still clenched in fury and frustration.

"We address a letter to the secretary of defense explaining the importance of quick action. Right after that, I'll drop-off the package in person. They will never expect that. There's a way to do this, and it's not on our own." She brought everything they had on Anand and the Big Data algorithm into her lap.

"What do you plan on doing, Jia?"

"We take it all to them, we hand it over and they do with it what they wish. They'll see what's going on, they'll understand that they have to stop the Islamic State. That's what our government does best, Greg, you know that. They combat terrorism and steal oil."

"What?"

"I'm kidding," she said, raising her hands above her head, "just thought I'd break the ice."

He didn't reply but scratched his chin. The Anonymous member rose from his chair and ambled to the door, but Greg didn't let him get there. He stood and blocked his path.

"You repeat anything you heard in this room, and I'll make you sorry. Understand me?" He pointed a finger under the guy's nose, and the geek flinched and nodded, shifting sideways. He scurried out a second later, tail firmly between his legs.

There was no doubt about it: he would've reported to a few senior members and they'd have been ousted. Now that Debra was gone, they didn't have any real connections within Anonymous.

"How macho," Jia commented. "Poor guy, you scared him half to death."

"It's him or us." He placed a hand on her shoulder and she reached up and touched it.

"Are you ready for this?" She rose from the chair. "We have to give up the algorithm too."

"If it's the only way, then I can't say no," he said, bitterness leaking through the acquiescence. "But what happens when you've done that? Jia, they'll never stop hunting us, never stop believing you're with the Gang of 8."

She didn't answer but walked to the door. He caught up with her and took her hand, and they went upstairs together.

An hour later, they were in front of the J. Edgar Hoover Building. Jia didn't wear sunglasses or anything black, she didn't even hide her face. She walked up to the front door and placed everything in the drop-box.

Then turned and walked back to the car. Greg revved the engine and she gave a small laugh, then slipped into the passenger seat.

"What now?"

"Now," Jia said, glancing back up at the building with a frown, "we take down the Gang of 8."

They drove off down the road, into freedom, but Jia couldn't help shrugging and glancing back. She was sure someone had seen them.

Someone was watching.

EPILOGUE

Jia looked the same as the pictures from her fake Facebook account.

He studied her, watching from a window on the seventh floor of the J. Edgar Hoover Building. Her hair was pulled back and her expression was determined, her lips drawn into a thin line.

He pulled on the dress shirt and buttoned it.

"They're here," a man said behind him.

"I know," he answered, putting on his cuff links.

"What do you want to do?"

The man – that was what he called himself in his mind because of the potential for anonymity – considered Jia for a long moment. Her movements were clipped and business-like. There was a brown envelope package in her hands, small enough to contain documents, but the way she carried it said it was precious.

Precious goods. Unlike Jia herself.

She hurried to the front of the building, just under his line of sight.

"Sir?" The voice grew concerned, the dulcet gravelly tone took on a sharp edge.

"Leave her. Let them go."

"Are you – " But the other one cut off short. He knew not to challenge the man's authority. Doing so would lead to a swift and painful death.

She reappeared without the package and jogged to the waiting car. The driver, Greg Davoli, revved the engine and she threw back her head and laughed. Very relaxed, but that was because she didn't know. She didn't foresee the storm on the horizon.

He studied his reflection in the window, his dark hair, the slant of his eyes, and smiled, exposing a row of perfectly even teeth.

Daniel Zang, that was what they called him. The man. That title was far better.

"Soon," the man said and the car sped off.

Jia could run, but she could never hide.

www.ingramcontent.com/pod-product-compliance
Lightning Source LLC
Chambersburg PA
CBHW030810310726
48980CB00006B/451/J

* 9 7 8 0 9 8 3 5 1 2 0 6 6 *